This book belongs to

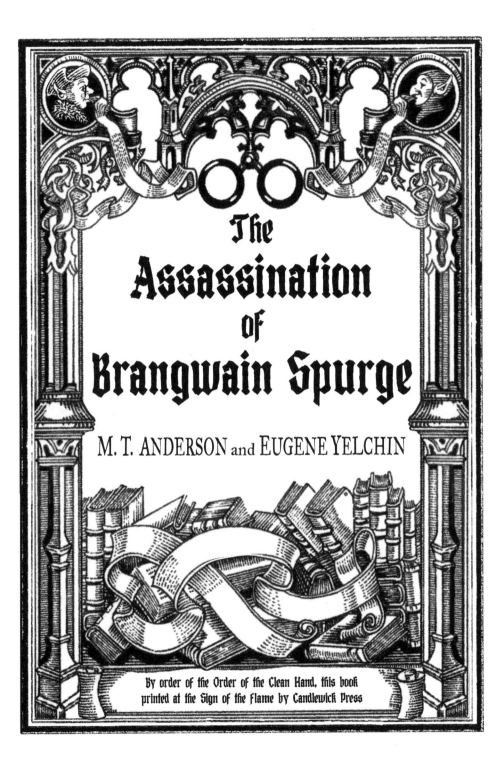

The
Assassination
of
Brangwain Spurge

M. T. ANDERSON and EUGENE YELCHIN

By order of the Order of the Clean Hand, this book printed at the Sign of the Flame by Candlewick Press

How can we ever tell what the world really looks like?

On a misty day, even the hills of Elfland are gray and dismal.

Look through a gemstone, and the dullest street sparkles.

I have had both my eyes put out by goblins,

and so, for me,

the world is profoundly dark.

— Lemuel of Chartibrande,
On the Elfin Sciences & Magical Arts

Chapter

1

Top Secret

Transmission

Chapter 2

From the Desk of Lord Ysoret Clivers
The Royal Order of the Clean Hand
Realm of Elfland

My Dear Friend,

You'll never believe who I shot out of a crossbow today.

Old Weedy Spurge from school — "the Weed."

We shot him into the dark heart of the kingdom of the goblins around noon.

Funny thing. I hadn't given the Weed a thought for ages and ages. At school, he was a bit of a drip. You remember: shrimpy little chap. Arms wobbly like kelp. Fishy sort of face. Terrible at the joust. Awful at hunting, too. Always getting bit by the elf-hounds. Frightened all the time. He walked around with his head hunched down on that scrawny little neck like he was about to be punched. Absolutely weedy, and named "Spurge," which is a weed. Hence, just called "the Weed," as you remember. And I didn't think about him for thirty years.

Well, imagine my gobsmacked surprise when one of the king's ministers told me they needed a historian to visit the goblin court of Ghohg the Evil One. Gave me a list to choose from. And there was his name, three down: Brangwain Spurge.

"By gum," says I, "it's old Weedy!"

I called him up to the palace for an interview. He teaches elfin history at the university. "Hello, Weeds," I said. "It's me, your old pal Clivers. Now a member of the Order of the Clean Hand."

You can't imagine how he's changed! No more head bobbing down low. Now he stands straight as a broom. Still looks a little weak in the arm, but there's nothing wobbly about him. Very proud and tall. Very stiff. I don't think the

chap could slouch if he wanted to. A wonderful transform-
ation. I was extremely impressed, and made no secret of it.

So I told him the mission: When they were digging the
king's new wading pool, they found some old, buried goblin
treasure — a giant gemstone carved with some kind of a story
on it. Typical goblin story: lots of beheadings. Disgusting.
But old, very old — maybe a thousand years old. The king
was thinking it could be given to Ghohg the Evil One, king
of the goblins, as a sign of goodwill and cultural exchange,
you know: a sign that elfish-goblin relations have improved
in the last five years, since the truce. A gesture. A handshake
across the Bonecruel Mountains.

Anything to stop them from taking up the sword and
flamethrower against us again and pouring out of those
mountains in their faceless swarms to burn our forests and
our homes.

The king's right-hand man tells me we need someone to
deliver this carved gemstone to the goblin citadel. A historian, someone who can explain its importance, its antiquity.
Someone who can talk with scholars there. Smooth things
over. "So, Weeds," I say, "would you be willing to serve your
country and head into the heart of the goblin kingdom —
from which no one has returned alive and whole for a hundred years or more? If so, old soap, just sign here at the X."

As I say, he's a cussed proud chap now, and so he didn't even so much as say "Yes, sir." Just stared at me — frowned — walked right to my desk, took the quill, and scribbled his name. I think he'll do grandly.

I do hope he will. All night, while the wife and I were at a Benefit Ball for Those Wounded by Griffins, I kept picturing the weedy little Weed at thirteen — not a muscle to him, flinching before he was hit, his big eyes shuddering whenever someone so much as looked at him — and then I'd think of the goblin kingdom. Mountains like broken teeth. Miles and miles of monster and goblin barbarian. Stinking pits. Cities like slaughterhouses. Rivers that run red. I told him that we would try to rescue him if something went wrong — but no elf has made it out of that dark land of mist and fire in living memory.

Well, except once during the most recent goblin war. April, five years ago. You may remember the Groozby Twelve, our crack commando team. They were sent into the goblin city of Tenebrion to try to map it out. Ten didn't even make it to the city walls. (Trolls, rock slides, a slithering fungus.) The other two were captured. Yes, they made it back here alive, but raving mad — unable to explain the horrors they'd seen, and not just because their tongues had been cut out. Their minds had been blasted. They were sent back over the mountains on a donkey with a head at each end. A two-headed donkey, fighting with itself even to walk in one direction. To mock us.

We do not know what lies behind those mountains. This is part of the Weed's mission — not just to deliver the carving, but to observe the goblin city and to tell us what he sees. He will be the first elf welcomed within those walls, surrounded by those goblin hordes and given a free pass to walk among them. Unless, of course, something goes wrong and they turn on him. They are known, after all, for their sudden anger, their enthusiastic violence, and their exquisite taste in torture.

I told him, "You'll be like one of those dusty old historians you were always reading, who went and visited the yeti in the frozen north or the dwarves under the ground and wrote a book about their customs and ways." But of course, it's not that simple.

I might as well admit that I'm a little worried about our old school chum. I'm jumpy about the Weed. Yes, the Evil One is expecting him — but is that necessarily a very good thing?

Do you want a bloodthirsty tyrant to know you're about to land bang on his doorstep?

I hope that when I sent the old chap off in the crossbow capsule, I wasn't shooting him toward his death.

I hope Ghohg will be impressed by our gift and our best wishes. Alas and all, though: We seek peace from a monster. The goblin nation squats there like a tarantula, waiting to leap and strike.

It is all in Weedy's hands now.

Remaining

    your friend,

Ysoret Clivers

Earl of Lunesse

Order of the Clean Hand

Peer of the Kingdom of the Elves

The night before Magister Brangwain Spurge was shot across the Bonecruel Mountains, Werfel the Archivist, goblin historian at the Court of the Mighty Ghohg, lay in bed under heaped blankets, unable to sleep. He turned to one side for a while, staring at the wall, and then turned to the other, staring at his bedroom door. His pillow was too hot and his hands were still cold.

He thought about the route the elfin scholar would take, spit out of a giant crossbow from the Royal Palace of Dwelholm.

He would be flying over fragrant forests where elves lived in tree houses, over rich meadows and pastures, over the dark pine slopes of the mountains . . . landing finally on the Plateau of Drume, by the walls of Tenebrion, the goblin capital.

A tiring journey, with lots of jolts, even if the crossbow capsule had lots of springs and cushions. *My poor visitor* — thought Werfel — *my poor visitor! He'll be exhausted. Hot. Bruised.*

It was Werfel's job to host the elfin emissary in the city, to take the scholar in as a guest in his own home. It was a huge responsibility. Elves were used to a certain luxury. Goose-down mattresses and stained glass windows. *My poor guest will be joggled to bits after slamming into the ground like that,* Werfel fretted.

And goblins had a strong code of hospitality. Once a goblin invited someone across the threshold into their home, it was their duty to serve and protect their guest, no matter what. Hospitality was holy.

Werfel sat up. He had to get to work plumping pillows and stocking the fruit bowl. It was no use trying to sleep, anyway. He was too excited.

He pulled at the tentacles on his face. Skardebek, his adorable pet icthyod, had clamped herself to his cheek, and she wasn't happy about being woken up. She angrily started to flap around the room, mewling in protest.

Werfel put on his glasses and stumped into the guest room to inspect it. Everything was ready. The bed was made. He had carefully turned back the counterpane, which was white as snow. Now he smoothed the sheets again, even though they were already smooth, and repositioned the hospitality chocolates on the pillow.

Did elves like chocolate? he wondered.

Who didn't?

Unless elves were allergic to it, like trolls or dogs. Perhaps he could ask discreetly when he met his guest, and slip in and grab the chocolates if it was a problem.

To make his guest feel at home, Werfel had hung his small collection of elfin art on the walls: ancient paintings in scarlet and gold of loving couples releasing doves in gardens, hunting in the forest, or playing healthy songs on zithers.

The day before, he had sent a few neighborhood children out to pick flowers for a bouquet on the nightstand. While the Plateau of Drume didn't offer much in the way of flowers, being swept by winds both hot and frigid, and often misty with volcanic fumes, the kids had managed to find some buttercups and saxifrage. Werfel knew nothing about flower arrangement, but he hoped that the handful of wildflowers he had propped up in the ceramic vase looked simple and attractive with a few sticks of dried ogresmace stuck in for contrast.

His ice cellar was stocked with meats and vegetables. He had a new barrel of rice and jars of pasta. What did elves eat? He did not know, exactly. Probably nothing but dainties: butterfly steaks and marigold salads.

Not true, he knew, shutting his eyes tight to try to calm himself down. During the recent wars against the elves, both sides had often stolen food from the other. Both sides had set fire to each other's fields and had rustled cattle through mountain passes.

Skardebek batted impatiently at the window. Now that she was awake, she was hungry. Werfel swung the casement open and let her out. She flew into the courtyard to find mold on compost. He saw her dancing around the neighbor's trash, delightedly kissing a rotten, black corncob.

The dawn was breaking over the uneven roofs and crooked chimneys of the city. The goblin historian decided he might as well get dressed. He went to the bathroom and scrubbed himself with disinfectants, scraping his hide with pumice stone. When he was clean, he pottered into his bedroom to pull his best academic robes out of the wardrobe.

He could not wait to meet Magister Spurge. He felt sick with excitement. Finally: contact with the enemy. With another scholar. With someone else who loved antiquity and beautiful things, and who shared his hope for this beleaguered world.

He had so many questions for him, and so much to show him. He wanted to introduce the elf to all the glories of goblin civilization: the Nawtle Caves, the dances of the Drovegas, the illuminated books of the Swallowed Emperor Period, the choirs singing the Lessons of Shadow, the race's ancient, melancholy epics recited to the accompaniment of the lute.

He even dreamed of being invited to travel to the white palace of Dwelholm by the visiting elfin historian. He would see the lush fields, the tall forests, and, most important, the fabled libraries, holding books no one in Tenebrion had ever read or even heard the names of. As Werfel combed the carpets to make sure the fringes all lay flat, he dreamed of the histories that could be written with the union of elfin and goblin knowledge.

He hoped that, even as he cleaned and prepared, his elfin guest was having a good and comfortable trip.

Chapter

4

Top Secret

Transmission

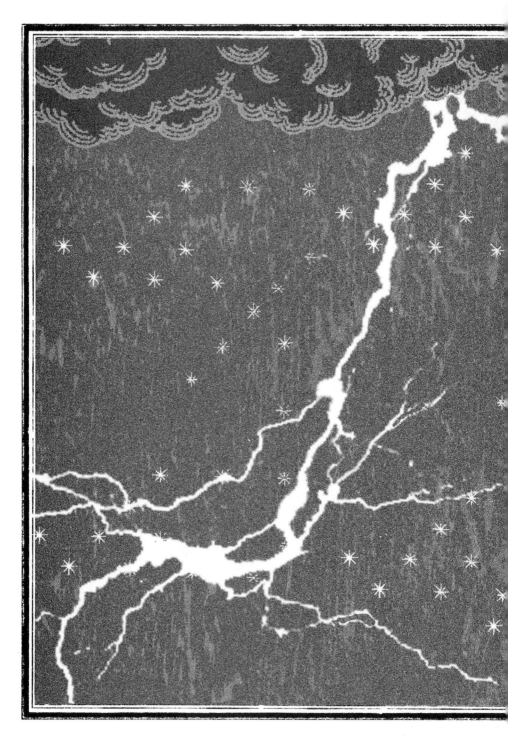

Chapter 5

By eleven o'clock in the morning, Werfel had walked up to Ghohg's fortress in the center of Tenebrion to wait for his elfin guest. Ghohg the Protector would not see the elf on the first day; that would show too much eagerness. Werfel had to meet the scholar first. He had to take him home and entertain him. Later, he was sure he would have to report on the scholar's interests and attitudes.

Werfel sat nervously in the palace's imperial archives, waiting to go down to the city gates and greet the guest. Skardebek fluttered softly around the room's rafters like an unsettled thought.

At around twelve thirty, word came from the far side of the mountains that sentinels had seen the capsule flying past. Ghohg had installed his own magical early-warning system: long, monstrous nerves that snaked through the hills and would jolt when a distant guard stomped on the other end. Over the next ten minutes, ministers followed the protest of alien nerves in fortresses across the Bonecruel Mountains and the Plateau of Drume. The capsule was soaring closer.

Werfel scurried up to the office of the Foreign Secretary so they could go out together to meet the visitor. When Werfel arrived, the Foreign Secretary was just giving the order for the three-headed wyvern to collect the capsule out of the sky and bring it gently, softly, safely down to the ground. They didn't want their elfin guest to be knocked around too much when the capsule landed.

The Foreign Secretary noticed Werfel shuffling in. "Ah, Archivist Werfel," she said with a tight smile. "Our guest will shortly be delivered. Let's prepare to go down to the Maw-Gate of Tenebrion to meet him."

Goblin guards posted along the battlements were watching the Plateau of Drume with telescopic distance-eyes. They turned left and right, scanning the sky.

One of them called out to the Foreign Secretary, "The three-headed wyvern's got him, madam!"

"Wonderful," said the Foreign Secretary. She bellowed, "Prepare the cheese platters!"

Werfel was so relieved. After all the preparations, he couldn't wait to finally meet the elfin scholar. He whispered to a goblin page boy in a ruff, "Start pedaling the motor for the champagne fountain." The champagne fountain, in the shape of a merman riding a dolphin, had not been used for years. It had taken a lot of time to clean and repair. The merman's puckered lips had been green with mold.

The boy bowed and scurried off to start the fountain gushing.

"Wait . . ." called the guard, uncertain. "Madam, there's something . . . It looks like the elf must be struggling in the capsule. . . ."

"What?"

"Oh, he's . . . Oh, no, madam!" The guard dropped the distance-eyes from his face. "He's jumped out of the capsule! He's falling. . . ."

The Foreign Secretary gulped and her large eyes widened.

"Come quickly, Archivist Werfel," she ordered. "We have to make sure he's safe. If that elf dies, it will be a diplomatic disaster." She shook her head.

Guards began rushing around and yelling things to one another. Observers on higher platforms bustled up and down ladders. Skardebek, startled by all the activity, pressed close to Werfel's neck, mewling. He held her comfortingly against his cheek with one hand while he picked up the skirts of his robes with the other, running as quickly as he could behind the Foreign Secretary.

Nothing could go wrong with this visit. This cultural exchange was important. Werfel was only too aware of that. No one wanted to think again of the suffering of the last war, the news of burning towers and legions dead. Stronger bonds had to be forged between elfin Dwelholm and goblin Tenebrion. This was his duty as a scholar and as a host. In some ways, his life depended on it.

A distant speck on the horizon, the elf fell through the air.

"He's falling into Lake Blunk!" shouted a lookout.

The Foreign Secretary rushed for the stairs, calling out to the guards she passed, "Patrol submarines! In the lake! Warn them!" She jabbed her finger into the air. "Pick him up! Get him to shore! Is this the season when the water serpents are hibernating or when they're hungry?"

Pathetically, with the creak of a tired motor, the fountain began to spit up champagne.

Chapter 6

Top Secret
Transmission

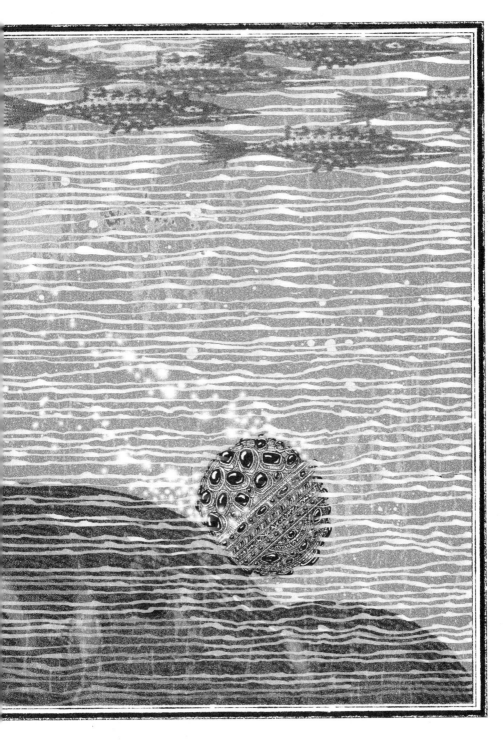

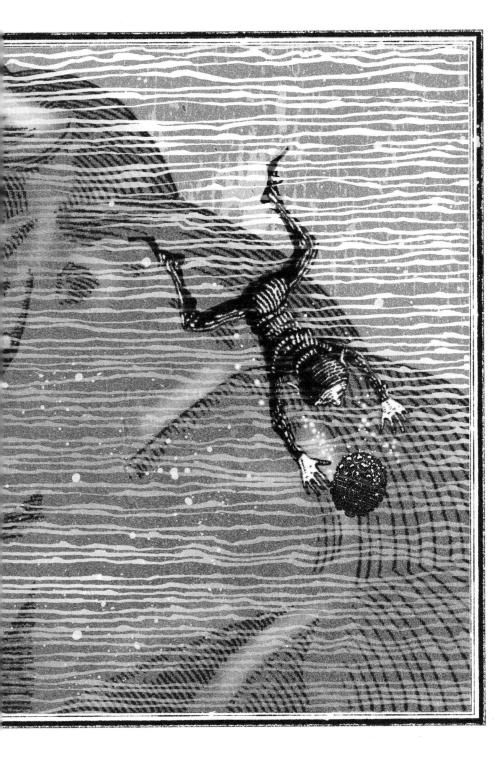

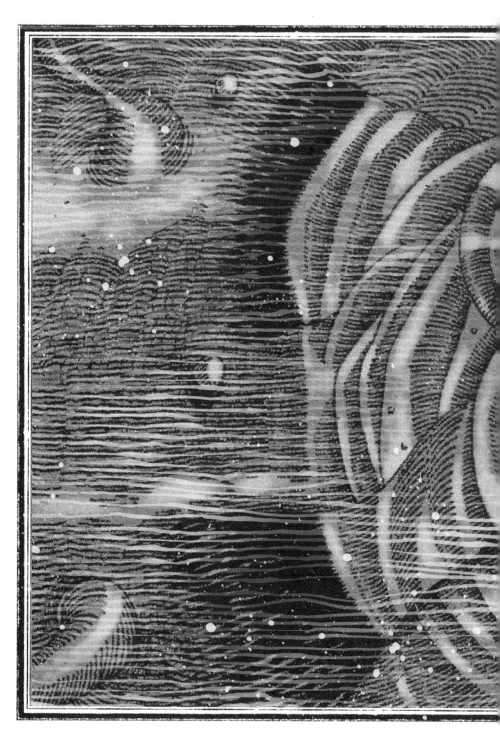

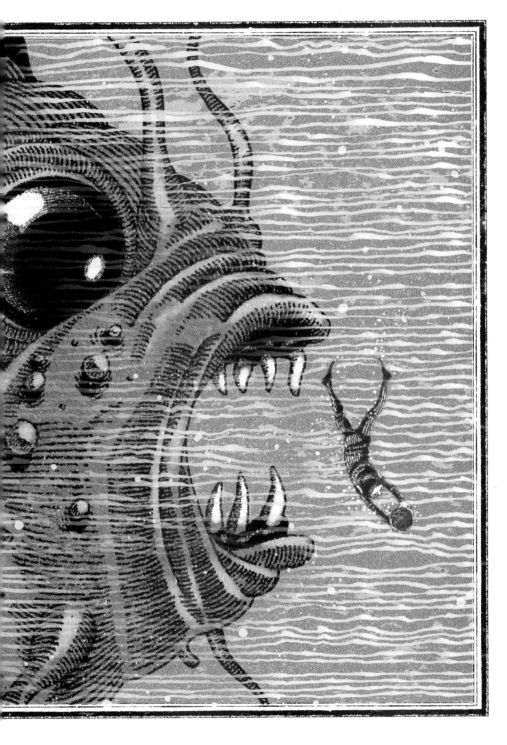

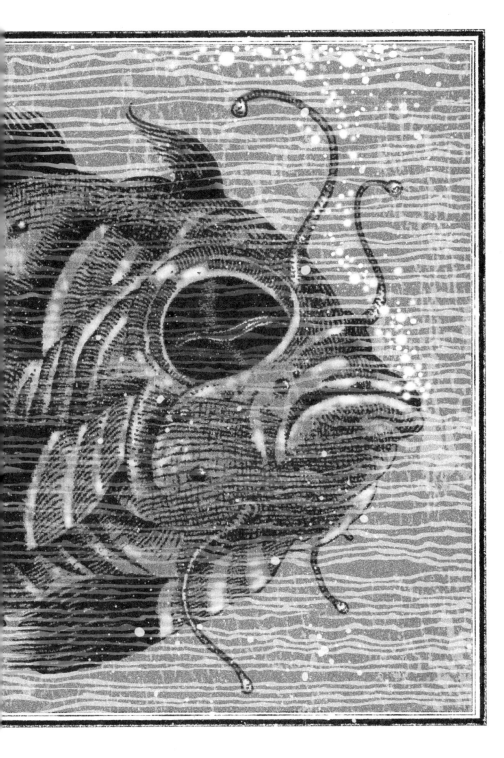

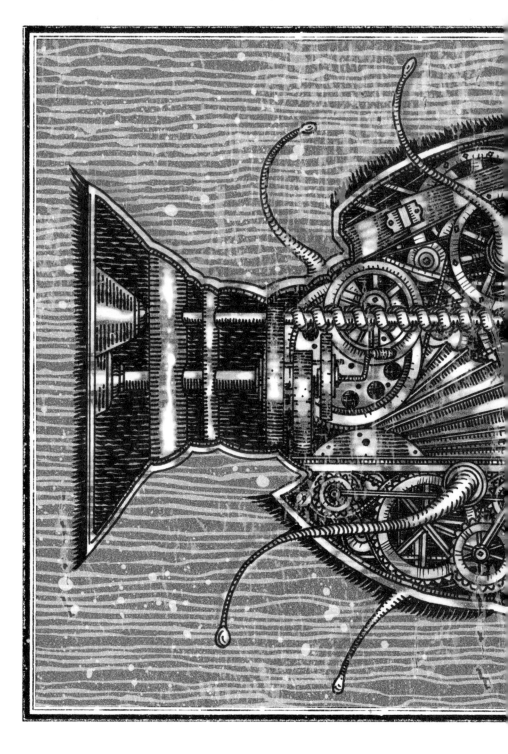

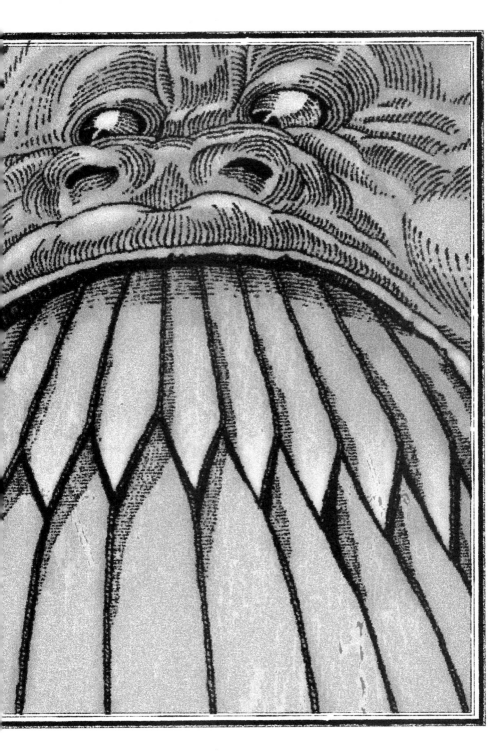

Chapter 7

Werfel stomped down the winding stairs after the Foreign Secretary, knees high. Skardebek flapped along beside him nervously.

He was not only worried about the safety of his invited guest. He wasn't just concerned about the political disaster if a servant of the elves drowned within sight of the palace. Everyone was worried about how the goblin overlord Ghohg would take it if this elfin visitor died by accident.

Ghohg often made people he was angry at disappear.

Werfel and the Foreign Secretary reached a landing where there was a giant metal orb covered with spikes next to a huge crank. An open hatch led into the orb.

"Come on, Archivist!" she urged. "Get in!"

Inside, there were velvet-padded benches bolted to the walls. Werfel, the Foreign Secretary, and several guards all took their seats and strapped themselves in. Outside, an attendant clanged the door shut. The Foreign Secretary pulled a chain, and a bell rang.

With that, the giant spiked sphere was released and dropped down a chute. A trench led straight from the palace toward the gates of the city. The orb skipped and rolled with a sound like thunder. Everyone was thrown around in their seats. Their arms flailed. The Foreign Secretary was yelling orders, but no one could hear her. Skardebek clutched Werfel's shoulder until she realized it was easier to hover in the middle of the rolling room, squealing.

The transport sphere plowed along the trench, past all the fortified city's defenses: walls, moats, machicolations, crossbow cannons, drawbridges, bristling spear pits, bladed gates, and giant mechanical grinders.

The sphere came to rest in a sand trap near the outer wall.

The Foreign Secretary was yelling in the sudden silence,

"—THE LORD HIGH GHOHG THAT WE WILL DELIVER THE ELF SAFELY, NO MATTER WHAT."

As Werfel emerged from the sphere, feeling dizzy and a little sick to his stomach, the Foreign Secretary was already talking to the watchmen at the gate.

It was the Maw-Gate, the great ceremonial entrance into the city of Tenebrion. It was cast out of bronze in the likeness of some forgotten god's snarling face. It confronted the bleak Plateau of Drume with angry brows and gnashing teeth.

Those teeth were sharp as swords. If there were an invading army, the Maw-Gate could grind them to pieces.

The Foreign Secretary had her arms crossed and clutched with worry. "It will be all right," she told herself. "One of the submarines delivered him to shore. Guards are bringing him up now."

It took fifteen minutes for the elfin emissary and his escort to reach the Maw-Gate.

Werfel could barely stand to wait. He was thrilled at the thought that his guest had almost arrived.

So much to talk about! So much to learn!

Bugles blew. Gears cranked. As the Maw-Gate opened, Werfel silently repeated his memorized speech to himself one more time: "GREETINGS to the traveler from the other side of the Bonecruel Mountains! GREETINGS to he who has flown through the skies to reach our gates! GREETINGS to the emissary of the kingdom of the elves! GREETINGS to the emissary from Elfland! And WELCOME to Tenebrion, our wondrous capital, home of our mighty overlord, Ghohg!"

The metal teeth creaked open. More and more of Brangwain Spurge could be seen — the weedy arms, a spherical box clutched to his chest.

Skardebek piped happily, eager to meet a new friend.

Giddy with enthusiasm, Werfel rushed forward, his arms spread wide.

"GREETINGS to —" he began.

He didn't get any further.

The elf had fainted backward.

"Oh," Werfel said.

The Foreign Secretary was horrified. "What have you done?" she hissed.

Chapter 8

हात wasn't at all the greeting I was expecting," said Werfel the Archivist, peering down at the fallen elf. "Should we slap him?"

The guards looked uneasily at one another. One took off his chain mail gauntlet.

"Absolutely not," said the Foreign Minister. "If you leave marks, it could cause an international incident. Archivist Werfel, take him collapsed to the room you've prepared for him. Watch him. Ensure that he recovers. Take good care of him."

Guards followed Werfel through the crooked streets with the emissary on a stretcher.

Magister Brangwain Spurge was tall, pale, and stringy. Thin, craggy. Even unconscious, he looked proud and haughty, but there was nothing to be afraid of. In the end, goblins and elves were not so different, were they? Werfel thought of the old saying: *Elf and goblin, we all have pointy ears.* So true.

"We'll tuck him in," said Werfel. He unlocked his front door. As the guards thumped past him into his house, he asked, "Oh — would any of you happen to know whether elves are allergic to chocolate? Little hospitality chocolates in the shape of scallop shells and ladybugs? Friendly little bonbons?"

The sergeant at arms gave him a long, unimpressed look and blinked slowly, once. It appeared the answer was no, she did not know about elves and chocolate.

They lay the ungainly elf on the guest bed and quietly shut the door.

"Thank you," said Werfel to each guard. "Thanks. Thank you. Thank you. Oh, thanks, really, thanks."

A short gray goblin in a lumpy gray tunic was standing at his side. "Archivist Werfel. I have been sent by the Minister of Secrets."

"It's kind of you to come by," Werfel whispered. He patted the air gently. "If you could speak quietly, our guest is asleep."

"Indeed," said the gray goblin, speaking just as loudly.

"When he wakes up, we want you to watch everything he does. We'll need a report."

"Of course, of course," said Werfel.

"There will be guards posted outside your house."

"Yes. As long as they don't make our guest feel in any way, you know, watched or unwelcome."

"Actually, he is watched and unwelcome."

Werfel raised a stern finger. "Not unwelcome! Not unwelcome! According to our ancient codes of hospitality, once he has crossed our threshold with our permission, it is our duty to keep him safe, or we lose all honor."

The gray goblin from the Ministry of Secrets paused by the door. "If he goes anywhere he's not supposed to, it's your honor that's on the line, and your life. I don't care about the safety of elves, Archivist Werfel. A lot of people I knew were killed by them."

The gray goblin frowned and left.

Werfel stewed and fretted. Distracted, he scratched Skardebek's back and combed his fingers through her little nest of tentacles.

When an hour had passed with no word from the elfin emissary, Werfel went up and listened at the door. He heard a faint crackling, a muttering.

He wondered what was going on.

Chapter

9

Top Secret
Transmission

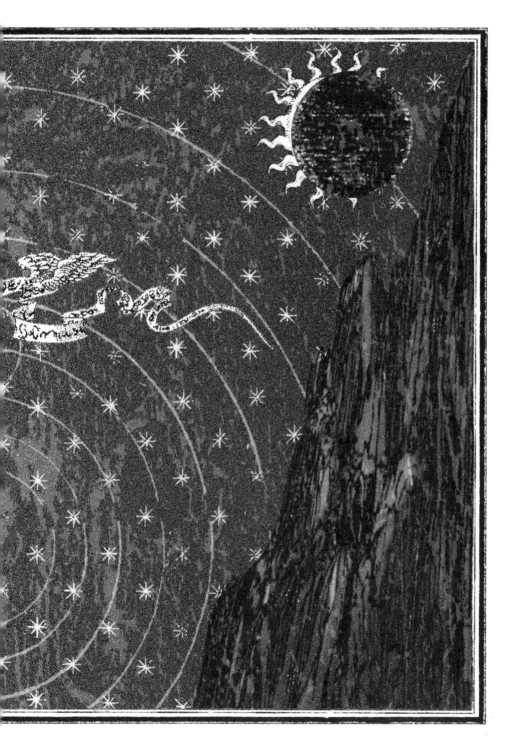

Chapter 10

ently, Werfel knocked on the guest room door.

The muttering stopped. Rustling. Then a loud voice, in Goblinish: "Enter!"

Werfel let himself in and bowed.

Magister Brangwain Spurge stood with dignity by the bed, as if posing for a statue of a conquering commander.

"I bring greetings," said Magister Spurge, "from the Elf King of Dwelholm, and look forward to the — That vermin!"

"Oh," exclaimed Werfel, twisting around to see where

Brangwain Spurge pointed. "That's just my icthyod, Skardebek." She settled on his shoulder and he nuzzled her with his lips. "She looks like a cuttlefish. But I call her my *cuddle*fish. Aren't you my little cuddlefish? Her name is Skardebek; I call her Bekky. She's a good little girl. She's an excellent little girl. The best little girl in school."

Brangwain Spurge made a face. He continued, "Why am I not standing before the Evil One?"

Werfel didn't understand. "Excuse the — Who?"

"The Evil One, Ghohg."

"Ah! You mean the mighty Ghohg, Friend of the People."

"I have a gift to deliver to him, a gemstone of unimaginable price, carved by your ancestors before your people crossed the Bonecruel Mountains into this land."

"The excellent Ghohg wishes me to look this splendid gift over for the next few days and talk with you about its history and provenance; and I will show you the historical sights of our fine city so you can take word of its glories back to Dwelholm."

"I have come to deliver a precious treasure to your dark master. I will give it only to him. Anything else would be beneath the dignity of the elfin nation."

Werfel played with the doorknob, twisting it backward and forward, listening to the click of the latch. "You shouldn't . . .

You know, Magister, you shouldn't expect too much from the Outworlder Ghohg. He's from another place."

"I, too, am from another place, and demand recognition."

"I mean a place much farther away. Another world. He is very unpredictable. Even his shape is difficult to figure out. His closest ministers can rarely tell his top from his bottom. You would not believe the number of servants who have been executed for trying to feed delicacies into the wrong end."

"I do not understand."

"Ghohg came to rule us from beyond. We do what he demands. He is very powerful. Also, very surprising."

"So when am I, royal emissary of the Elf King, to be presented before him?"

"When he asks to see us. I am sure he's very anxious to meet you, in his own way. Who could not be, esteemed guest?" (Werfel bowed again, nervously.) "We wait on Ghohg's divine whim. For the moment, I will show you the city. Tonight, we have been invited to dinner by the du Burgh family, a very wealthy and prominent goblin clan — the height of refinement — who are famous for their knowledge of elfin culture. They have an elf in their family past. Through marriage. They are extremely eager to entertain you."

"I cannot leave the gemstone. I must protect it with my

life." Brangwain Spurge reached out and touched the metal box that held the gem.

"Would you like to carry it with you?" Werfel asked. "You could take it to the feast. I am sure that the du Burgh family would treasure a glimpse of it. A historical artifact so precious. I can barely wait to see it myself, and to talk to you about it, and discuss what it might tell us about the ancient history of our two races, and —"

"I will not take it out of its casket."

Werfel didn't really know how to react to this. It was his job to inspect the gemstone. But it was also his duty to make his houseguest feel safe and welcome. For the moment, he simply said, "As you wish, esteemed guest." He bowed. "Though . . . I will need to look at it before it is delivered to our overlord, Ghohg."

"I have been given orders to keep it safe in its casket until I can deliver it to Ghohg myself. It is priceless."

This stymied Werfel. Things were not going very well. So he said the only thing he could think of. "May I give you any refreshments? Would you like some fruit?" he offered. "I have many varieties in a bowl laid out for your pleasure. Apples, oranges, pears."

"Give me a pear."

"The pears are bruised on one side. I just turned the bruised sides down. They are for show. Maybe you would like an apple."

Brangwain Spurge nodded. "I would like an apple."

"The apples are very good apples."

Werfel went to fetch the bowl. He was glad Magister Spurge was at least interested in the apples. Fruit was very rare in the kingdom of the goblins. Most of it had to be imported from the human lands to the south. There were no orchards on the Plateau of Drume—not like in Elfland, famous for its fruits and its vineyards.

Werfel held out the bowl to his guest and watched Brangwain Spurge pluck up an apple and bite.

"Good, isn't it? Yes, chew fully. Swallow. Another bite! Chew again, esteemed guest. Whenever you're ready, we'll head to the Tower du Burgh. We'll be accompanied by guards. For your safety, of course — your safety. Chew once more."

Magister Spurge nodded. Taking another crunchy bite, he followed Werfel into the sitting room. Werfel busied himself putting on his formal hood, while Brangwain Spurge stopped chewing and stared in horror at a set of knobbly gray-green garments draped on frames by the windows.

"And what are those?" he asked through a throat constricted with disgust.

"Oh!" Werfel laughed. "My skins. My previous skins. When

we shed every few years, we keep them." He picked up the limp hand of his ten-year-old self. "Good memories," he said. "It's important to see who you're growing into and who you used to be."

"Disgusting," said Brangwain Spurge under his breath. "Of course I've read that you shed your skins . . . but not that you keep them lying around."

Werfel reminded himself that Brangwain Spurge was his guest, and was probably just going to take a day or two to get used to the ways of goblins. Soon, Werfel was sure, they would be best friends.

"The skins of goblins are treasured possessions!" said Werfel. "They are our history. Some families who like crafts even fill them with dried beans and pose them in favorite attitudes — a big hug, for example, or a beloved picnic."

Brangwain Spurge put down his apple with a sour twist to his mouth. "I am surprised they don't decay."

"Oh, no! Some remain around for generations. When I was small, my parents still had my great-grandmother's last skin. Imagine: I could touch her hand with — with this hand!" he exclaimed, lifting up the wilted fingers of his own kid skin. "Imagine the privilege!"

He waited for the elf to admire the family tradition, but Brangwain Spurge just stared with repulsion at Werfel's deflated past faces. To Werfel, they were the whole record of who he had been. He was proud of them, and he felt a little embarrassed that his guest saw them as nothing but disgusting.

So Werfel tried to change the subject. "Are you ready to go?" he asked. "It seems like you are done with your apple."

"I would like a chain," said Brangwain Spurge, "to hang the sacred box holding the gemstone around my neck so I can carry it with me."

"Won't that be very, ah, heavy, my pleasant companion?"

"It is a burden I carry for the king of Elfland."

Werfel shrugged. "I might have something on my bicycle. One minute." He went down into his cellar and brought up a chain. Together, they draped it around the elf's neck and ran it through the handle on the metal box.

"Is that satisfactory, most excellent visitor?"

The chain rattled. The box was huge and hung heavily. Brangwain Spurge stooped slightly under the weight.

Werfel told himself, *It will just take a little time for him to trust us, and then we will speak more openly.* "Comfortable? Then off we go!" he crowed.

He unbolted the front door. Brangwain Spurge left the rest of his apple behind on a table, uneaten.

Then they walked outside, and Brangwain Spurge stumbled backward in shock.

Werfel's neighborhood was crammed, loud, and rowdy. A horde of children scampered over the cobbles, playing incomprehensible games with chalk. A man was hanging out wet laundry on his balcony while calling out threats to his neighbor. A goblin lady was heading home from work with gold chains hanging from ear to huge, pointed ear. Her wooden high heels rapped the stone street. A pageant float of priests went by slowly, pulled in their cart by a group of beasts. A candy vendor was barking about sweet, chewy manna that had crystallized on the stalagmites of Thulm. From down the lane, the racket of tinsmiths and coppersmiths filled the air like flashes of fire. Even the crows on the roofs were arguing.

Over the noise and bustle, Werfel yelled, "I have been so looking forward to showing you our city!"

He always loved that moment when he passed into the narrow streets and lanes either from the coolness and quiet of a house or from the trenches that led into and out of the heart of Tenebrion. The city's fortress walls were so plain, so blank, and then he would go through a gate — and everywhere, Werfel thought joyously, everywhere there was life.

Brangwain Spurge looked pale. He winced at the noise. He looked ridiculous with the giant, fancy box creaking back and forth on the chain around his neck.

Werfel pitied the poor elf, who was looking so out of place. He sang out cheerfully, "This way!"

Two guards moved to follow Werfel and his guest.

A ring of children gathered around them, peering up at the elf's weird, pasty face.

"Hey, four-eyes!" called a woman in a window. "Werfel! I see you stopped reading those big dull books long enough to actually leave the house!"

"Only to be ambushed by this army of little jerks! Your awful spawn! How many do you have now? Can you remember which ones are yours? The brats are gawping at my guest!"

The woman laughed. "They're just shocked someone as boring as you could actually find a friend!"

Werfel gave a joyous cackle and waved.

As they moved on through the crowd, Brangwain Spurge muttered, "What an awful woman."

It was Werfel's turn to be shocked. "She's one of my dearest friends. Her family is like my family."

"Then why did you mock her for the number of her children?"

Werfel chuckled. "Oh, that! It is an old goblin custom: The closer you are with someone, the more you make fun of them. It is a sign of how friendly you are."

"To say offensive, personal things?"

"If you said them to a complete stranger, they would fight you in a duel to the death." He waved to a young man they passed and called out, "Ugly as usual, Rogbert!"

The young man waved back and sang out with a smile, "My gorge fills with hate for you, you ancient, decayed sack of manure!"

Werfel clapped his hands together. "As you can see, I love the people in my neighborhood very much. I would die for them, to keep them safe. But when we pass beyond this gate, I must hide my smile. The people beyond do not know me."

The city of Tenebrion was built in rings, with tall walls

separating them. The closer a neighborhood was to the palace at the center, the more deluxe it was, and the more expensive the houses and mansions became.

Werfel didn't say anything, because he did not want his guest to feel unwelcome, but he knew that once they got beyond the bounds of his own neighborhood, prying eyes would be glaring at the elfin guest. So many goblins had lost brothers, sisters, mothers, fathers, sons, and daughters in the wars. Werfel was glad they had the two guards pacing behind them. Otherwise, violence might break out.

Even with the guards to show they were on official business, Werfel knew that as they walked across bridges and through winding streets, informants for the Ministry of Secrets were rushing to tattle on him, as if walking beside an elf were itself a crime.

They were watched everywhere.

Werfel led Brangwain Spurge through the crowded streets, pointing out sights: "There's the Temple of Great Rugwith, built more than three hundred years ago"; "Here's our big smash-puck stadium, where we hold our national sport. Smash-puck. Perhaps you would like to watch a game? We can sit several rows back so you won't get as much blood on you"; "Oh, there are some of our goblin scouts dressed up for a military parade. Aren't they adorable in their little armor? Those little faces in those little helmets?"; "Here's a memorial statue to all of the goblins who fell in the Third Elf War. Carved with such sadness."

Silently, Brangwain Spurge stared at each monument and temple as if committing them to memory.

The two scholars and their guards passed through market crowds. Goblins made wide circles to avoid brushing against the elf.

They made a point, however, of bashing against his goblin guide, Werfel, as if by accident. The mob elbowed the archivist in passing. They slammed him with their arms. They stepped on his pointed shoes. A few said, "Ohhhh, sorry," but in voices wiry with irony.

"Heh," said Werfel, hobbling a little from a crushed toe. "Streets really are crowded today! As you can see, Tenebrion is a lively city! A wonderful place to — ow, eh — raise a family or livestock."

The scrawny elf frowned.

"This on the left is the Noble Hall of Justice, where we hold trials. And see over there, over that wall? That pointy, crystal spire is the Well of Lightning."

The elf goggled at the weird structure. "The Well of Lightning?"

"Oh, yes," said Werfel, delighted that his guest seemed interested. "It's the source of much of our wizardly power. Its power lights the whole city."

"What a miraculous device. Could we go see it close up?"

"It is off-limits and guarded by vork. You are right that it is miraculous, wise and clever guest. It was brought here by Ghohg the Protector when he first arrived among us."

"How fascinating."

"You will find many fascinating sights in bright Tenebrion. Here, for example, is a statue of a cat who used to put out fires."

Werfel kept talking in this way until he looked around and realized that his guest was no longer by his side. Just as he was about to panic, however, the crowd parted, and Brangwain Spurge stumbled out, looking harried.

Just in time, too: They had arrived at the Tower du Burgh. They were met by a whole rank of goblin trumpeters dressed in elfin livery, playing a harsh goblin fanfare.

This was a nice change from the abuse they'd suffered on the walk over.

The doors were flung open.

And goblin figures rushed toward them.

Chapter 12

Top Secret Transmission

Long Live Our Leader

Ghokg-The Protector

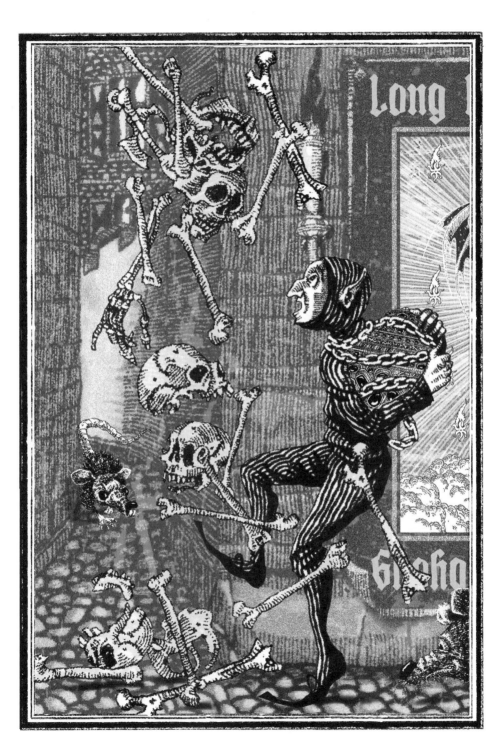

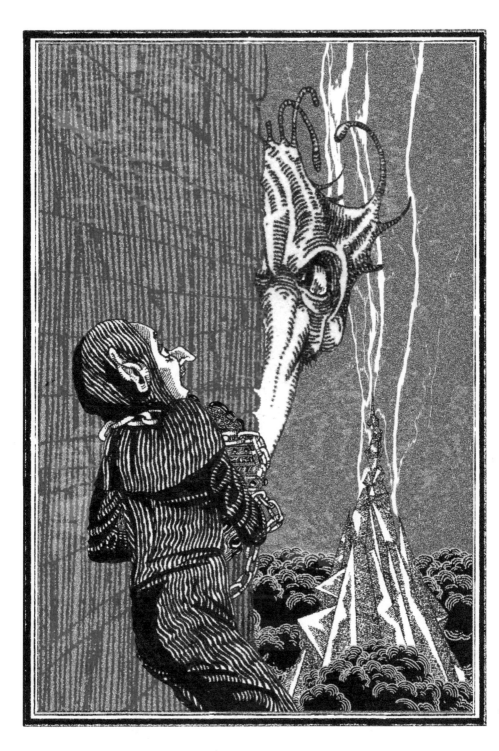

Chapter

13

It was the whole wealthy du Burgh family rushing out to greet them.

"We have been so looking forward to meeting you," cried the Lady du Burgh in Goblinish, clutching both of Brangwain Spurge's hands in hers, pressing her nails into his palms. She winked, then switched to somewhat imperfect Elven: "It us pleasure to have stuff you full with food inconveniently, Magister Spurge."

"Isn't that wonderful?" said Werfel in his perfect Elven.

"Lady du Burgh and her whole family have learned the language of your people. They want you to feel absolutely at home here."

The elfin guest just stared at her with his mouth open.

Lady du Burgh smiled graciously and said, "I punch you with me house."

Werfel said, "I think she means she hands her house over to you for the evening. Her house is your house."

She nodded. "I punch you with me house hard, many time." Then, in Goblinish: "Is that right?"

"Almost, Lady du Burgh," said Werfel, bowing. "But of course, the beauty of your voice makes it hard to concentrate on the words alone."

She laughed and called for her children, who all danced up, dressed weirdly in little elfin frocks. "Say hello to Magister Spurge as I taught you," she prompted, and they chanted in Elven, "We give you fat greetings, sir! Sprayed all over!"

Werfel saw, delighted, that the whole of the du Burgh family had dressed in fine elfin clothing for the party. They had clearly gone to a lot of trouble: Elfin clothes did not fit well on goblin bodies, and so they had safety pins clenching the sleeves on and seams pulled open so they could breathe.

"Lady du Burgh," said Werfel, "you are a wonder. You are the queen of hospitality."

They proceeded up the stairs, led by Regibald du Burgh,

Lady du Burgh's cousin, a muscly goblin gentleman who looked like he could crush the head of a dragon in his bare hands. But he was gentle with Spurge, saying quietly to him in Goblinish, "My cousin loves the culture of your people. It is our hope, elfin guest Spurge, that this is just the first contact between our two kingdoms. I, for one, am going to try right now to forget all the elves I killed in all sorts of ways during the war, and I'm not going to think of all of my friends you people shot and stabbed and cut apart. Oh, and burned from the air. And imprisoned without food. Tonight, my cousin just wants you to feel comfortable and welcome."

Brangwain Spurge looked confused, as if perhaps he didn't feel comfortable and welcome yet.

In the grand dining room, the noble family had laid out elfin delicacies in heavy silver dishes. There were arches of spun sugar, towers of pastry, basted birds posed for flight. Werfel knew it must have taken them days to find all these delights and prepare them in their kitchens. He was almost in tears with gratitude.

"Lady du Burgh!" he exclaimed. "Ah! Ah! Magister Spurge, look at this feast! Every detail correct!"

"Well," said Lady du Burgh conspiratorially, "not every little detail, of course, despite our best efforts. We apologize that we had to make a few substitutions, Archivist. We couldn't get actual hummingbirds in the Bonecruel Mountains, for instance, so we had to make do with a flight of baked carrion crows. But you'll find the bluebell velouté sauce and the ambrosia reduction absolutely authentic. You won't notice a thing!" And then, in her best broken Elven, she said to her guest, "Take part! I demanding you plant you face in meat and starts to bite!" She steered Magister Spurge forward. "Gnaw, new unhomely person — gnaw!"

Spurge went forward to the table with great dignity and sat down. The other guests — knights and generals, scholars of history, a few artists and merchants — went to take their seats, too.

Lady du Burgh whispered to Werfel, "Do you think he is impressed?"

They sneaked a glance at the elf. Spurge looked dumbfounded.

Werfel smiled broadly. "He must be. You have thought about every detail."

"A real elf . . . " she said in wonder. "Just think: This morning, he ate breakfast in the white castle of Dwelholm, surrounded by all the knights of Elfland."

"But it is a greater honor to dine as a guest of Lady du Burgh."

Lady du Burgh laughed and then asked quietly, "How is my Elven, really?"

"Flawless, madam, as you are yourself."

She cocked an eyebrow at him. "You know me better than to lie, you old toad."

Werfel could not believe his happiness. To be called an old toad by the Lady du Burgh! An old toad! Tonight he was rocketing up the social ladder.

He smiled shyly. "Awful," he admitted. "It sounds like you are choking a donkey."

She laughed and threw her arm around him. She scrunched his shoulders up tight and said, "You are a ghastly, dry little man!"

Werfel bowed in pleasure and went to rejoin his guest. Lady du Burgh's cousin, the hulking warrior Regibald, was leaning over Spurge, saying, "I myself was very gentle with the elves during the war." He put his hand over his heart. "When most goblins took elfin prisoners, they cut off their arms at the elbow. Not me, sir. No. Even after I saw the horrors of the massacre at Bludgely, I always cut off your people's hands right at the wrists." He smiled broadly.

Spurge looked ill. In Elven, Spurge said to Werfel, "This man is terrible."

Werfel said, "Sir du Burgh is a soldier, not a diplomat. You must excuse him."

Regibald asked with irritation, "What are you two chatting about?"

"Pleasantries," said Werfel. "The Elven language is excellent for party trifles."

Regibald said, "I was just telling Magister Spurge I was very fair with my elfin prisoners of war. For example, when I had to execute knights, I made sure their heads came off in one blow of the ax. Quick and clean."

Werfel bowed. "I am sure our esteemed guest appreciates your efficiency and mercy — justice as sharp and sure as the edge of your ax."

He led Spurge off by the elbow before the elf could protest.

Spurge demanded, "Are they mocking me? Teasing me? Laughing about the torture of my people while they're dressed in our chopped-up clothes?"

"Oh, no! No, Magister! They're only trying to please you!"

"How could they possibly please me by —"

A trumpet sounded, and everyone took their seats. Lady du Burgh picked up a porcelain plate and smashed it on the floor, the traditional cue for a formal dinner to start. The goblins, with delight, began pulling apart the food in front of them.

It was delicious. Werfel was in heaven. He had often read about elfin food in books but had never tried most of the dishes. He chatted with everyone around him and grinned. He looked at the smiles on the faces of the kids, the grease on the cheeks of the other guests, and mused that this was what goblin life should be like all the time: eating, laughing, ribbing. He said quietly to Magister Spurge, "There is nothing better than being with friends, is there? As our hostess put it, planting you face in meat and starts to bite?"

He expected a laugh. Spurge did not speak, and seemed to choke a little bit on his dinner.

Werfel put down the largest of his set of knives.

"Are you all right, esteemed guest?"

Spurge made a face and removed a wad from his mouth, curling it in his napkin.

Lady du Burgh was watching the emissary carefully. She clearly had noted that he was not enjoying his dinner.

"Magister Spurge," she said, "perhaps to settle your stomach, a little music?" She made a gesture, and a bard was wheeled out on a platform. "He will sing several of your country's elfin tunes we are particularly fond of in this house." She waved her hand in the air.

The bard began to belt out a popular song from Dwelholm called "Your Blond Locks (Shine Like Some of the Sun)."

Immediately, Werfel and Lady du Burgh noticed Spurge wincing. The elfin song was clearly not going over well.

Werfel ducked his head and, worried about offending someone, suggested softly, "Sorry, Your Ladyship, sorry, sorry, but maybe, Your Ladyship, we might ask the bard to play a goblinish tune? One that the singer is more familiar with? Our esteemed guest may prefer to hear our music, since he has deigned to come so far to our prosperous land."

After the wooden, desperate performance of the elfin song, Lady du Burgh announced, "Now the bard will play one of the great epic songs of the goblin people, sung while we dine: 'The Death-Song of Walgund,' written a thousand years ago. It is music that shall be heard as long as there are goblins to play it, as long as warts and pointy ears persist on this earth."

The bard looked grateful he didn't have to sing in Elven anymore. He closed his eyes for a long time. The table grew silent. People shifted quietly on their cushions or pushed their plates away so they wouldn't clank during the singing.

The bard plucked a few notes on his harpsicophone. Werfel immediately was swept up by the ancient tune, as heartbreaking and familiar as his mother's tears. In Old Goblinish, it was a lament sung by the hero Walgund in the days following the destruction of his city by King Degravaunt of the Elves, when the elfin armies overran the forests. The song described the home that they had lost forever: the orchards, the cool lakes, the warm forests, the green fields. The plucking was odd and untuned, as it should be in "The Death-Song of Walgund," as if the melody were exiled even from itself. The bard was superb; Werfel could not believe the delicacy of his performance, the way he shaded certain words and made others glow like memories of morning.

"What is this song?" Magister Spurge asked in a whisper. "I cannot understand it."

Werfel, trying to make him feel better, said, "Oh, of course not — it's in Old Goblinish. Very difficult even for goblin students to understand. Of course! Of course."

"It is some kind of a battle cry?"

Werfel said, "Oh, no, no, no! Well — well, yes, it is about the attack by King Degravaunt on the goblin cities of the forest a thousand years ago. But it is a love song, a memory of a place that no longer exists except in yearning, where we all wish to —"

"You call this entertaining a guest?" Magister Spurge asked. "You ask your bard to sing a war ballad about killing my people? I can hear the noise in his voice!"

"Well," said Werfel, "Old Goblinish is a somewhat harsh-sounding language, somewhat heavy on the plosives, but it's not really —"

"You call that hospitality?" Spurge's voice was getting a little loud. "To sing a song about attacking King Degravaunt, our greatest hero, the founder of our elfin nation?"

Werfel looked anxiously around the table at the other guests. They all were glaring at the elf. Lady du Burgh looked furious. Werfel put a warning hand on Spurge's wrist — but Spurge continued, "I am a representative of the Elf King! His Majesty, may he live forever, is a direct descendant of King Degravaunt." He rose violently to his feet. The bard's harpsicophone clanged to a stop. Spurge ranted, "It was Degravaunt who cleansed the forests of darkness!"

"Friendly visitor," Werfel said quietly, "the forests were not darker when we lived there. 'The Death-Song' remembers our forests as being bright and warm and full of sweet smells."

But Spurge was not even listening. "This wretched kingdom is exactly as I had always heard it would be! A barbarian nation interested in nothing but war! With no culture of its own! So you must borrow ours, the culture of the most refined race in this world — the culture of the greatest, noblest, and fairest court to ever raise turret to the clouds — and your fine food is nothing but elfin food, made disgusting and grotesque, and your fine clothes are nothing but elfin fashion, made ugly and strange on your bestial bodies, and you mock our great heroes in your songs! Your country is exactly as we were warned it would be!"

Werfel felt sick to his stomach. He was sure there had been a misunderstanding somewhere. He thought there was a good chance this meal would end in violence. But for the moment, he had to protect his guest. There was not a goblin around the table who wasn't thinking about challenging the elf to fight a duel to the death. Lady du Burgh was no longer glaring at Spurge. She was examining her set of knives.

"Lady du . . . Lady du Burgh, we really must be going; it's after . . . some o'clock. Sorry. Sorry. So sorry. Guards?" The guards came forward to stand on either side of Magister Spurge.

The rest of the goblins at the table rose, and Werfel could not tell whether it was out of politeness or menace. They had their hands on their utensils.

"Well, Lady du Burgh. It was a truly splendid party, if, ah, if, ah, if this 'old toad' may say so."

Lady du Burgh narrowed her eyes. "I do not believe I ever called you that," she said. "Or if I did, I apologize." Slowly, carefully, she told him, "I will never call you an old toad again, esteemed guest."

Werfel shuddered at the words "esteemed guest." It was a terrible thing to be called by one who was your friend. He wondered how long he would live after Magister Spurge went back to his own country.

The two scholars backed away, with the guards keeping an eye on the dinner party.

The knives in guests' hands dripped on the floor.

Chapter

14

The walk home seemed endless. The night was dark, and goblins' eyes glimmered in windows and alleyways. The guards watched carefully for attackers. The elf was silent now, and seemed to have learned his lesson. He clearly was terrified for his life.

Werfel was too watchful and frightened himself to calm his guest down. He tried the occasional, "You would enjoy the carvings on this building, if it were light enough to see them," or "Down that way is a splendid clothier." But the weight of everything going wrong was too heavy. He could not carry the conversation alone.

So they got back to his house in misery and went inside.

Werfel locked and bolted his front door.

He did not know how he would face the neighbors if word spread. An elf speaking out against a noblewoman in her own home. It was a disaster.

The elfin emissary went into the guest room and shut the door. Werfel heard the scholar slide a chair under the knob.

Werfel called the little icthyod to him, and she danced on his shoulder. He stroked her and held her tight against his cheek. She was the only thing that cared about him, it seemed. She didn't understand what was wrong, and that, strangely, was a comfort to him. "Oh, Skardebek. Bekky, old girl. Bekky. The smelliest little girl to ever fly through the window."

As he went carefully to bed, Werfel heard muttering in the elf's room again, just like earlier.

He pressed his ear against the guest room door. He could not make out the words.

He knelt down and looked through the keyhole.

The elf was lying flat as a board, muttering a spell.

Werfel could tell it was a spell because the elf was floating several inches above the bed, surrounded by crackling sparks.

Werfel wondered what he had gotten himself into.

He did not sleep that night, but sat up in his roof garden, watching his city, his beloved, dangerous city, and worrying about how he would live through the next day.

From Lord Spymaster Ysoret Clivers,
Order of the Clean Hand
To Lord General Baligant, Commander in Chief of the
Grand Army of Elfland

My Lord General,

Our scholar-diplomat, Magister Brangwain Spurge, code name: "The Weed," has at this point been in the goblin capital of Tenebrion for eighteen hours.

No, in reply to your question, he did not exactly arrive safely. There were dangers. You know: A three-headed wyvern. A fall into a serpent-infested mountain lake. And the goblins themselves, of course, which are nasty little things. His host looks like he'd as soon eat your face as shake your hand. Pointy teeth and whatnot. The usual hideous goblin mug.

As the Lord High Chancellor may have told you, my Order has a wizardy sort of device to get messages from our people out in the field. Whenever Weedy gets an hour alone and away from prying goblin eyes, he goes into a kind of trance and then imagines what he wants to show us, whatever he's seen. Pictures it deucedly hard. Then he says the magic words, and, presto change-o . . . his thoughts come whizzing back across the Bonecruel Mountains. Our boys back here in the white marble halls of the Order of the Clean Hand have a sort of receiver attached to a printing press. Big machine made of brass, silver, gold, and dragon bone. They lay down a sheet of paper on the printing press, clamp the press closed, and when they open it, there's a picture of whatever the Weed has been thinking about, inked in black and white.

Of course, General, it's not perfect. It's not exactly what

he sees. It's whatever he pictures in his mind's eye. It's his image of things. So we rely on him to observe well.

That's why we're so glad we've chosen the old Weed. Not only does he speak Goblinish like someone served up with a side of warts and claws, but he'll know what he's looking at. He's a historian, an expert on the goblin-elf wars of centuries past. Give him time, General.

The Lord High Chancellor has said we can lend you some of the images he has already sent back.

What can we see from the images he's sent? First, Tenebrion's a nasty place, of course, and the goblins live in utter squalor, filth, and poverty. They're mean, gruesome little barbarians. There's a military unit, for example — they look like little more than kids. Marching, as you'll see, General: hup two three four and all that. Preparing to tromp out and lay waste to our fair kingdom. Just as we suspected. Goblins care about nothing but warfare. And when they're not setting up to attack us and lay the torch to our homes, they're aping our fine ways, eating elfin foods, trying to be just like us. Unsuccessfully, of course. It's pathetic.

Look in particular at the awful goblin women — brutish, roaring things. We know that goblin women fight and rule alongside their men — hulking, ugly beasts, dreadfully unlike the beauties of our own elfin aristocracy, who are bred for their delicacy to be ornaments to society. This is yet another example of goblin savagery, their lack of nobility and chivalry.

And catch a sore eyeful of the poster of the Evil One himself, Ghohg. We can't even make out what the awful thing is. During the war, we questioned captured goblin soldiers, and they told us rumors that Ghohg is not from this world but is some kind of awful gosh-knows-what from gosh-knows-where. It looks as if that could be true. That's the monstrosity we're up against.

Now, the most interesting of these pictures is the pointy business behind that wall. We think that must be the fabled Well of Lightning. The source of a lot of the goblins' magical power. That, My Lord General, was one of the things we asked the Weed to look at most specifically. We told him to sneak around it and try to figure out how it works. This is just a stroll-by, but we're counting on him to get back there and take a closer look in the next day or two. We need a little nibble of recon, real spying — and then he'll send us images of what he sees.

Be patient, General. Isn't all this frightfully interesting for you?

There will be more soon. I have every confidence in the Weed.

Ysoret Clivers, Lord Spymaster
Earl of Lunesse
Order of the Clean Hand

Chapter 16

The next several days were not easy for Werfel. He was very eager to show the elfin emissary around, but nothing ever seemed to make Magister Brangwain Spurge happy.

Since Spurge had not appreciated the du Burghs' attempts to cook elfin cuisine, Werfel took Spurge out to a fine restaurant and treated him to local goblin delicacies: steaks of the fierce gorrelaptor sizzling in plum sauce, and mosses swimming in the thick, peppery cheeses of the Burgash Mountain area. Smoked plesiosaur. Crunchy fried tendons from the bludge.

All the varieties of pickle the Plateau of Drume was known for, stored away for the months when the snow was heaped too deep to grow any vegetables, or for the late summer when the firestorms blew through and goblins had to crouch inside their houses for days, going out only if wrapped in aluminum caftans. Pickles of all kinds, rich with the spices that grew on the mountainsides. Pickles kept in dim crypts and basements by every family, each with their own recipe passed down from generation to generation.

Spurge gagged. He pushed his plate away. He murmured that everything was too spicy. Too smoky. Too heavy. Too greasy. All the flavors were too strong.

Werfel assumed Spurge would be interested in seeing what the goblins thought about the recent wars against the elves, so the two went to a memorial up on the battlements of Tenebrion. It was a statue of an old goblin couple, holding out their arms yearningly to a son and a daughter across the courtyard, both of whom were wide-eyed and dead as ghosts, elfin spears of stone broken in their bodies. It was a very powerful set of statues.

Spurge found it tasteless. "If you didn't want to lose soldiers, you shouldn't have started a war."

"We didn't start a war," Werfel almost said, but he remembered he was the host and it would be impolite to argue. So he said nothing and just tried to smile.

Since that first night, when he'd seen Spurge in a trance, Werfel had realized that his guest was sending messages of some kind back to Dwelholm. That only made Werfel more determined to be an excellent host. It was especially important that the elf should be impressed by Tenebrion's wonders and hospitality.

It didn't help that in general, Magister Spurge did not seem very talkative. Werfel had dreamed they would spend the days and nights trading stories of history and notes about their different cultures — fellow scholars!

But Spurge answered all Werfel's polite questions in the shortest way possible.

"So," asked Werfel, "where did you study history? Ganulant University? Ullbridge? The Invisible College?"

"Mm," said Spurge.

"And before that? As a boy, you were at Dwelholm Noble Academy?"

"Yes," said Spurge. And then silence.

"It must have been fascinating, to rub elbows with all the glorious flower of elfin nobility and knighthood." Werfel waited for an answer.

Spurge looked at him and said nothing.

Werfel didn't know what to do. He could not keep talking if his guest would neither fully answer him nor ask questions back.

Werfel's mother had often told him that it made sense to ask questions about other people. "It's polite. It shows you're interested," his mother said. "People will like you more, because almost everyone enjoys talking about themselves. And it's more fun than talking about yourself. You already know about yourself. You'll never hear interesting stories if you don't ask questions. And there are interesting stories everywhere. Even the most boring person has one interesting story."

So Werfel tried asking Spurge about Dwelholm. "I have always wanted to see the famous libraries of the elves. In particular, I've heard that there's something called the Library of the Order of the Clean Hand that has illustrated books you can find nowhere else in the world. Very rare. So rare. A wonderful story. Is that true?"

Spurge's eyes went left. Then they went right. He licked his lips. No answer.

Most frustrating of all, Werfel could tell that he and the elf were very similar in a lot of ways. He knew that both of them had come from poor families. Both of them had been sent on scholarships to schools run for the children of the powerful. Both of them had spent their lives studying the history of goblin-elf conflicts.

So Werfel tried to show Spurge the glories of goblin culture and history. He introduced him to the cream of goblin society, and to dancers, singers, painters, schoolteachers, and merchants with an amateur love of history, the kindest and most curious people he knew in Tenebrion. Everyone was gracious and thrilled to meet the elf emissary. But Spurge hardly spoke. He sat, looking conceited and uncomfortable, straight as a broom.

Werfel took him to hear a choir sing the Lessons of Darkness in the Temple of Rugwith. During the quiet parts, Spurge looked bored. During the loud, furious parts, Spurge blinked and looked offended by all the noise.

Still, as Werfel rushed his guest from event to event, he vowed *I will show him the best Tenebrion has to offer. Then he will have to send home dazzling reports of our city, its culture, and its hospitality!*

Werfel thought: *What could possibly go wrong . . . ?*

Chapter

17

Top Secret

Transmission

Chapter 18

'll try to show him that goblins can be fun! Werfel thought, so during a furious thunderstorm he took Spurge out on the streets to watch the children jumping from rooftop to rooftop with their elaborate metal wands, trying to catch lightning bolts.

"Look!" Werfel said. "Isn't this scene joyous?"

Apparently Spurge was not convinced.

Spurge actually seemed somewhat distressed by the mother-daughter Flower Day Parade. Was the singing of "The March of the Blossoms" too loud? Or maybe elves were not familiar with living dragonvine and everblooming basilisk's tongue? Werfel's elfin guest certainly seemed nervous about the dance of the flowers, supposed to represent the wonderful bond between goblins and the natural world. Whenever the plants threw the dancers up into the air or kissed a woman with sloppy affection, the elf flinched as though her head were being bitten off.

Magister Spurge did not seem much more pleased by the solemn Museum of Eminent Skins. He did not take any interest in the discarded skins of famous goblin heroes and actors, despite all of the interesting dioramas. At the end of the tour, he did not even want to pet the Slough of Vertigrin the Wise for good luck.

It seemed Werfel couldn't win.

In fact, there was only one event Brangwain Spurge seemed to enjoy — and it involved his life being threatened.

It happened this way:

One evening when they were eating at a restaurant under a bridge, Werfel looked up and saw Lady du Burgh's cousin Regibald du Burgh come in. As Werfel watched, Regibald spotted the visiting elf and immediately scowled. He walked over to their table and just stood there and glared. He must have stopped in for a bite to eat after playing wargames at the battle yard. He was dressed in light armor. He was sweaty and covered in dirt and grass clippings. He did not smell good. He had several friends with him, and they all looked as if they could get mean.

Werfel could not believe that, on top of everything else, he now had to be threatened by one of Tenebrion's most powerful noble families on account of Spurge's bad behavior.

"Oh, if it isn't Regibald du Burgh," said Werfel weakly, hoping nothing disastrous was about to happen. "I cannot believe I am sitting here at this restaurant, eating food, when I could simply sit at home and remember the taste of that feast at your cousin Lady du Burgh's home last week. I could roll the memory of that exquisite food back and forth on my tongue." He pushed his plate away from him in a show of disgust. "Other food, get away! I wish only to remember the generosity and kindness of Lady du Burgh!"

Regibald du Burgh sat down heavily at their table.

He jabbed his thumb at Magister Spurge and grunted, "Why hasn't this pale night-worm crawled back to the hole he came from?"

Werfel watched several moods pass over Spurge's face: First, surprise. Then, outrage. Then, clearly, a thought occurred to Magister Spurge . . . that this must be one of those goblin insults that show budding friendship. The elfin emissary tried to smile a little, like he could take a joke.

Unfortunately, it wasn't a joke. Regibald was in the mood for murder, trying to pick a fight.

Werfel shook his head slightly to warn his guest. He started to stammer something loud about the weather, but the elf was already stiffly trying his best to make friends: "I would say that it's good to see you again, Mr. du Burgh, but it's not, since you smell like a horse carcass rotting out on the Plateau of Drume." He smiled, proud of himself.

Regibald du Burgh began breathing heavily. He said, "I'm going to pull you apart, elf. I'm going to pull off each one of those thin, spindly, pale arms. But you'll still be alive."

Spurge looked to Werfel to check how things were going. Werfel felt sick.

"That was a little extreme," said Spurge. "As we're not great pals yet, why don't you start by making fun of my nose?"

"I'm going to grate the flesh of your throat off you like cheese."

"See, is that really the spirit of the thing? Maybe I don't understand."

Werfel gathered his courage and piped up: "Regibald du Burgh, this elf is my guest and my responsibility, and any violence you wish to do to him must first be done to me." He tried to sound brave, but his voice wavered.

"Did I do the insulting correctly?" Spurge asked Werfel, completely unaware that the knives being drawn were for him. "Mr. du Burgh started it, after all."

But du Burgh growled, "Elves start everything." He leaned forward so his spittle would hit the emissary's chicken pie. "Like the recent war."

Spurge folded his napkin and laid it beside his plate. "Young man," he said, "I hate to correct you, when we have just become fast friends, but the recent war was started when the goblin horde, for no reason at all, swept out of the Bonecruel Mountains and destroyed the border town of Plurenton."

Werfel was in a panic. There was nothing Spurge could do that would be worse than arguing about the recent war and reminding everyone how many of their friends and family had been killed fighting the elves.

Regibald argued, "That's what your king said. Your stinking Elf King. That's his story. But he might not have told you that a few days earlier, his guards led a night attack on one of our border castles. Massacred everyone. Just like an elf would: Sneaky. Cowardly. Tricky. On griffin-back. With the whole town of Plurenton behind them."

Werfel, with a kind of hysterical cheerfulness, said, "Isn't it so fascinating how in different countries, we have different views of the same events? This is one of the things that historians can do, clearing up these little misunderstandings in an atmosphere of friendly debate, where —"

"That is absolutely not true," said Spurge scornfully. "I have seen the official documents, and they said nothing about —"

"So you're calling me a liar?"

Werfel took Spurge's arm. "We should not talk about the war. We all lost so much. . . ."

Spurge said haughtily, "You wouldn't have lost anything if you hadn't started it."

"Magister Spurge, Magister Spurge, Magister Spurge, come with me," Werfel urged, tugging the scholar's arm. "Magister Spurge?"

Spurge, yanked by his host, stumbled away from the table. At that moment, Regibald du Burgh leapt to his feet. He and his friends pulled out their weapons and drew into a formation.

"Who are these others?" asked Spurge.

To Werfel's horror, Regibald du Burgh and his friends began throwing their knives, hurling their axes.

Spurge yelped and ducked.

purge looked up when he discovered that for some reason, nothing had chopped his head in half. There was a clanking of weaponry.

The young men were juggling. They were catching one another's weapons, tossing them back and forth in a display of strength and agility. All the while, their eyes were fixed murderously on Magister Spurge, emissary of the elves.

It was the traditional Dance of Announcement. Warriors did it at the beginning of battles to intimidate one another. The next thing that happened was that they carved you up so quickly you never felt it.

Unless they wanted you to feel it. Over several hours.

The blades spun back and forth, glittering in the restaurant's torchlight. Regibald du Burgh and his buddies were showing off their might in battle.

Spurge's plate was hacked exactly in half. One half of it flew onto the floor.

Waiters ran into the kitchen.

Spurge stood his ground proudly. Werfel was impressed. Spurge looked ready to die with honor.

Werfel bleated, "Magister Spurge is not only under my protection!" Regibald du Burgh caught a battle-ax in midair and waited. Werfel explained, "He is under the protection of our beloved ruler, Ghohg. He is an official guest of the state."

The two guards who followed them everywhere stepped forward.

Regibald sneered. "He won't defend himself?"

Werfel bowed low. "When he has returned to his country, you may do to me what you would have done to him."

"He's a guest of our mighty Ghohg?"

"Indeed he is."

Irritated, Regibald said, "Long live His Otherworldly Majesty."

"Yes. Long live him," said Werfel, and bowed.

Regibald du Burgh, with death in his eyes, nodded and backed out of the restaurant. His friends followed.

Werfel could barely breathe.

The guards stood firm on either side of the table.

When Werfel turned, he saw that Spurge was already seated again. The elfin scholar had picked up the half of his chicken pie that remained on the table and was eating it. He plucked out a pickle and, for the first time, ate with gusto.

"A wonderful display of the goblin martial arts," the visitor said happily. "It's so generous of Mr. du Burgh to arrange this show of your quaint local folkways just for me. I have heard elfin knights describe this from the battlefield, but I never thought I'd see it myself. Now, tell me: If I am correct, usually it leads directly into battle? When not done out of friendship, like this?"

Werfel collapsed into his chair. His arms were limp. His heart still raced. "Why did you do that?" he found himself saying. "Why did you talk about the war that way? We've all lost family and friends!"

"I cannot stand inaccuracy."

Werfel looked straight at his guest. He could not help himself. He said: "My own beloved girlfriend died in the war. She died on the elfin front. Blanchepon was her name. She died."

At that, for the first time, he thought he saw Magister

Spurge look ashamed. It was just a brief glimpse. Spurge's lips moved, as if to say "I'm sorry." But he said nothing.

Wearily, Werfel tried to become a good host again. He could not believe he had made his guest feel guilt. "Eat your pie, Magister Spurge. In an hour we will go see the goblin play *Lovebirds in the Cavern of Doom*. I have purchased tickets."

Spurge played with the half of his chicken pie that hadn't been chopped by a battle-ax. Embarrassed, he said, "When you next see Regibald du Burgh, please apologize on my behalf."

When I next see Regibald du Burgh, Werfel thought, *he will be wielding a two-handed sword and cutting off my head. It will be the last thing I'll see.*

"And thank him," said Spurge, "for the war dance. Let him know it was very instructive."

Chapter 20

From Lord Spymaster Ysoret Clivers,
Order of the Clean Hand
To His Royal Highness, the King of Elfland

Your Majesty,

We receive daily updates from the spy we call "the Weed,"
who is embedded, or one might say implanted, in darkest
Tenebrion.

Before we shot the Weed out of the crossbow, we told
him in no uncertain terms, "Look, Weedy, we need you to

snoop around the Well of Lightning. It's the source of quite a bit of goblin magic." And so we wait, Your Highness. We get pictures of the usual goblin insanity — their squabbling, their gruesome torture chambers, a load of their women being eaten by carnivorous plants — but we have got nothing but the merest sketch of the enchanted Well.

We at the Order of the Clean Hand are even more impatient than you are, Your Highness.

I here must admit that I've known old Weedy since we were at school together, and he was never a particularly brave chap. Right from the beginning, he was a poor, scrawny little blighter, always weeping during his first week in the dormitory because he wasn't at home with his mommy and daddy anymore. Scared of anyone with money and a noble title. Didn't make many friends, as you can imagine, Your High-ho. And from then on, he was always frightened when we burned his desk with him tied to it, or when, as a jolly little jape, the other prefects and I dragged him down to the crypt and forced him to eat grave-worms or have his pale little head kicked in.

He was, even then, the Weed: unwanted by anyone. As we frequently reminded him.

So he may be up to his old Weedy tricks, too frightened to really spy for us.

Is this a problem, Your Highness? Of course not; have faith in your humble Order of the Clean Hand. We know our business, my king and liege and chum and all that.

There are the other plans I have made for the Weed. I shall say no more. I went down today to talk to Lord General Baligant about the operation.

For the moment, Your Maj, we'll wait for the images of the Well of Lightning. Then we move on quickly to the next step.

As for this afternoon: centaur polo at 2:30. Would you care to place some bets?

One shall see you at the hippodrome,

Ysoret Clivers, Lord Spymaster
Earl of Lunesse
Order of the Clean Hand

Chapter 21

The next day, Brangwain Spurge disappeared.

It happened this way:

Werfel thought that Spurge, as a visiting historian, would be interested in historical drama, so he took him to the twenty-hour-long opera *The Bitter Defeat of Grudvid, and What Followed Afterward.*

Of course, the opera, like everything else, totally failed to entertain the elf.

At about hour six, Spurge leaned over to him and whispered, "How long does this torture go on?"

"About twenty hours, give or take, esteemed guest, depending on whether they choose the happy or sad ending."

Spurge's eyes shot one way and then the other. "I am afraid my stomach has become unsettled from too much pickle."

"A thousand regrets! What can we do?"

"Nothing, Archivist Werfel. Please take no trouble over me. Remain seated."

"You, too, esteemed guest!"

"I must go find a privy."

"Allow me to ask the management."

"No, no. I will go alone. I may not be back for some time."

"Really, I must ease the way for you."

"Many thanks, Archivist, but I don't wish to cause a stir."

Werfel held up his hand in blessing. "May peace and calm descend upon your gut like a gentle mist on the gurgling river rapids."

"I beg you not to talk about running water. Excuse me."

The elf half stood and worked his way along the row, slipping out of the theater.

Werfel turned his attention back to the opera. He hoped that poor Spurge felt better soon.

Onstage, Blulinda sang a love duet with Gorgigard while they fought with wooden swords. Then there were some dancing gnomes. Almost invisible from a distance, like some kind of trained-mouse act, but very charming.

By the time Werfel noticed that Spurge had not returned, an hour had passed.

The goblin checked his watch and panicked. He wriggled and stooped past the rest of the audience. "Excuse me. Excuse me. Excuse me, honored sir." He went out into the lobby. He ran up the stone stairs to the privies. All the doors but one were open.

He knocked. No sound.

"Magister Spurge? Excellent friend?" No answer. "Perhaps you have fallen asleep with your head upon your knees?" He banged on the door. "MAGISTER SPURGE!"

Nothing.

Now Werfel was the one who felt sick to his stomach. . . . If something had happened to Spurge, he would be held responsible and perhaps executed. And if Spurge hadn't gone into the toilets at all but had made a run for it . . . For what? . . . Spurge couldn't get very far. The two guards were standing at the front doors of the theater.

He rushed downstairs. He popped his head out of the front doors. The two guards assigned to him and Spurge were standing stiffly, waiting with their pikes.

"Hello," Werfel said. "Have you seen Magister Spurge?"

They turned to look at him. "Is there a problem, Archivist?"

"Oh, no. No, no, no, no. No, no, no, no, no, no, no, no, no. That is just what there isn't. He must have stepped into the gents' room."

"We'll check," said a guard.

"No need! No earthly need! You just rest yourselves. Can I buy you something at the snack shop?"

He slammed the door shut and ran back up to the privies. He knew Spurge couldn't have left through the front doors. So he must still be inside the privy.

Unless, realized Werfel . . . Oh, no.

Werfel yanked furiously on the closed privy door. The door was latched from the inside. He pounded helplessly.

Thinking quickly, he reached into his pocket and pulled out a quill pen. Carefully, he scraped the pen up and down in between the door frame and the door. With the tip of the quill, he gently lifted the latch.

The door swung open.

Inside was a tiny closet with a wooden seat that had a hole in it.

There was no sign of the elf anywhere.

Brangwain Spurge had disappeared.

194

Chapter

22

Top Secret Transmission

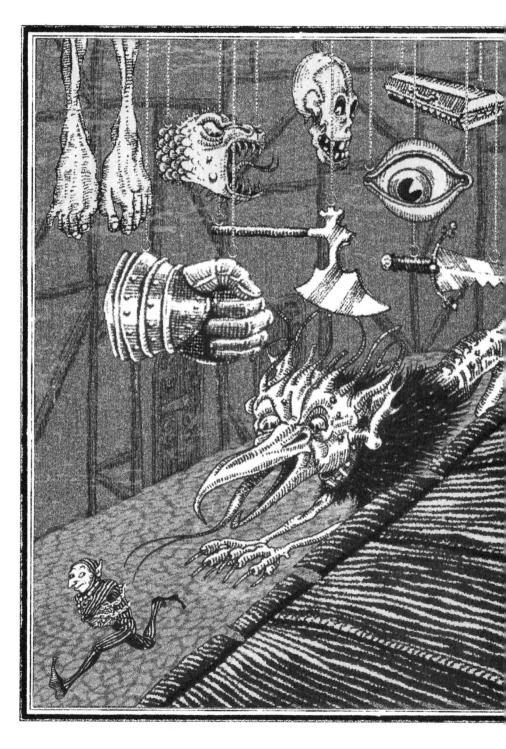

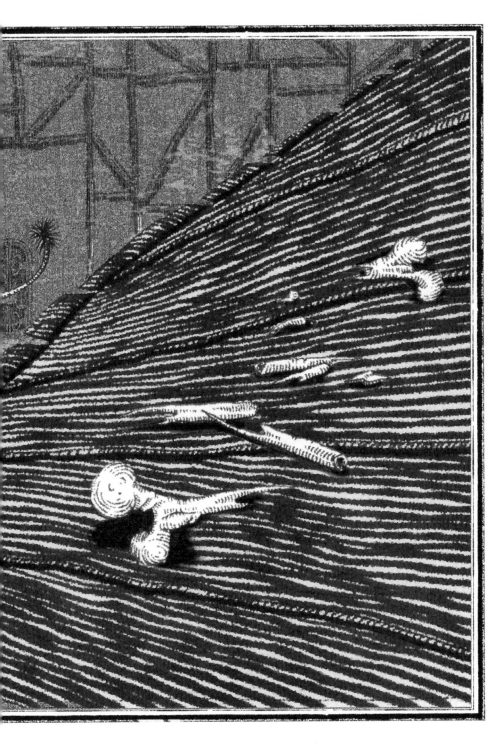

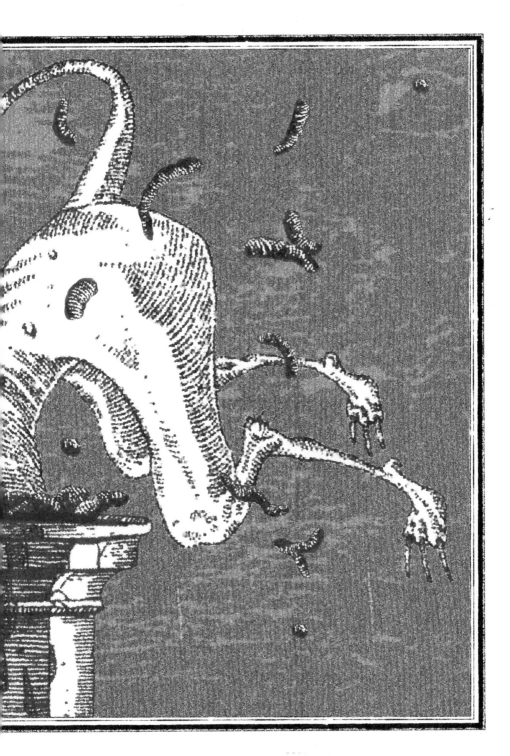

Chapter 23

Werfel was in a panic. He could feel his blood drain from his blotchy face as he stared at the toilet. He was worried about his guest's safety, but also about his own. The secret police would not be happy that he had lost his elf.

He crouched over the privy and looked down. Someone could easily crawl out the hole and jump down into the street below. Spurge must be off spying.

He stuck his head through the hole and peered up and down the alley. At the far end of the street, there were signs for various posh businesses: an optician, a doctor, a kitchenware boutique, a maker of ladies' fine opera gloves. But no sign of anyone.

He was furious. Spurge had betrayed his trust.

When he looked up from the toilet, shifting on his knees, he saw a wealthy goblin woman draped in strings of pearls glaring at him.

"Just vomiting, madam," he apologized. "That shrieking harpy who's playing Blulinda really should not be singing." He stood up and, with dignity, left the privy.

He walked back and forth in the gallery, wondering what he was going to do. If he told the guards that Spurge was gone, the game was up. He would be in disgrace, perhaps in danger of beheading for his negligence.

On the other hand, what if he didn't tell the guards and they found out? Then his crime would be even worse. Treason.

To tell or not to tell? To tell or not to tell? The question flew in desperate circles around his head.

Someone tapped him on the shoulder.

Spurge?

He turned.

It was one of the secret police guards.

"Are you sure there isn't a problem, Archivist? You seem kind of worried."

"Worried?"

The guard looked up and down the gallery. "Where is the elf?"

"The elf," said Werfel. "The elf!"

He didn't know what else to say. He could feel his mouth clapping open and shut idiotically.

"Where is he?" asked the guard, perplexed.

"I am worried about him."

The guard prepared his pike for combat. "What's wrong?"

Werfel gave a long, drawn-out sigh. That bought him several seconds. Then he said, "Oh, nothing that you can solve with your weapon. No, no. No! He has a tetchy tummy. He ate a bad pickle. Elves have a delicate inner system. All their tubes and intestines and things. Made for eating gold leaf and bluebells. Ha, ha. He is in the toilet. He'll be in there for a while, I suspect." Werfel smiled. "A long, long while."

The guard looked suspicious. "Should I check on him?"

"Certainly not, my fastidious friend! You cannot simply bang on the door of an elfin emissary while he does his business! For the elves, all aspects of life are an art. Even on the toilet, they think of nothing but beauty and elegance. Knocking on the door would be like hurling a fry-pan at a great artist painting a masterpiece of a sunset on distant hills."

". . . Distant hills?"

"Why don't you go and take my seat in the theater for the

moment, while I wait for the elf? Surely you want to see *The Bitter Defeat of Grudvid*. It is a classic of eighth-century goblin culture."

The guard looked skeptical.

"Sit back. Relax. Sunflower seeds from the snack bar?"

The guard made up his mind. "I'm going to check the toilets." He stomped off toward the stairs.

"No! No, no! You'll disturb him!" Werfel bounded up the steps, plucking at the guard's sleeve. "Don't forget about the art! The elfin art of living! Like a landscape painting of a sunset! With the ancient forests steeped in evening glow, and the brown cliffs, and the spires — the spires of a distant castle, catching the last rays and turning a glorious gold!"

The guard turned on him. "What are you hiding, Archivist? What are you trying to hide from me?"

The guard made his way to the privy doors. Several were shut.

"Don't!" squeaked Werfel.

The guard knocked on the first. A woman called out, "Occupied!"

"No!" Werfel pleaded.

The guard knocked on the second. A boy called out, "Yeah?"

"Stop!" said Werfel, grabbing the guard and trying to pull him away.

The guard leaned forward and, with his pike, whammed the third and final closed door.

"Please!" sobbed Werfel. "Please!"

The door opened.

"You needn't make such a ruckus," said Brangwain Spurge, stepping out of the privy, drenched in sweat. "The garderobe is all yours."

From the toilet came a hideous, screeching yowl of anger.

With his nose in the air, Magister Spurge marched past the two goblins and headed back to his seat.

Chapter 24

Werfel sat furiously next to Brangwain Spurge, but he hardly heard the opera. He had spent his life studying elfin culture, but at that moment, he hated elves. All elves.

He thought about the goblin losses during the recent elfin war. Border towns devastated. Stories of atrocities and massacres. Temples ruined. Houses blasted. Goblin children fleeing griffin-riders through fields, screaming and zigzagging as the elfin knights dipped lower, hurling magic flame from their flying mounts in the black, smoke-smogged skies.

Spurge sat there, smelling absolutely foul. Werfel couldn't stand the stench.

He couldn't be polite any longer. He hissed, "What were you doing? Where were you?"

For a moment, Spurge actually looked sheepish. "I was . . . I just needed to be alone."

"Where did you go?"

"I just wandered around the streets for a few minutes. I had to breathe. I am a poor scholar — I am not used to guards following my every move."

Werfel stared into his eyes. "Are you telling me the truth?"

"Yes," the elf answered without hesitation.

"I hope so. You know that since I'm your host, my fate is tied to yours."

Neither of them was paying attention to the opera anymore. There was a fake boat onstage and the chorus was jumping on and off of it, singing, "Huzzah!" They all swung around the mast.

"If you're not enjoying the opera," said Werfel, "there is no reason to keep sitting here like a couple of grapefruits rotted to the shelf."

"Fine," said Spurge, and they both got up and left.

They stepped out of the theater and just kept on walking without saying another word to each other. The guards fell in behind them.

They wandered down through the levels of the city. People

stared at the elf like they always did, but frankly, Werfel didn't care.

He stopped once, in the middle of the street, to say only "Don't abuse my hospitality!"

Then he stomped onward. Brangwain Spurge looked kind of surprised.

They got back to the goblin's house. When they passed Werfel's neighbors, he didn't even stop to insult them. He went right in and shut the front door behind them.

The two guards stood out on the street, holding their pikes.

Spurge stood at the door to the guest room. "Good night, Werfel."

Werfel didn't face him. "Good night," he said, in the least friendly way he could.

"I know that you are . . . trying," said the elf. "And I thank you for it."

"'Trying,'" Werfel repeated poisonously. As if goblins somehow had to *try* to impress an elf.

"I said 'Thank you.'"

"I heard you say it. Those words."

Werfel heard the door click closed.

Once Spurge was shut up in the guest room and the whole house was in shadow, Werfel went and sat next to one of his skins. He had shed it seven years before, in the middle of the war against the elves. When he had worn it, he had been a different man: younger, happier.

He touched the husk of his younger face and thought about his beloved Blanchepon. He wished she could have been there with him to help with his guest. He imagined Blanchepon — sweet, stormy Blanchepon — whispering support while they scurried to make sure that there was always a fine wine for the elf for dinner and healthy whole-grain toast for breakfast. "Don't worry about that stick of an elf," she would have said. "He'll be out of our hair soon. Not that you have much hair, you dry, balding old lizard." Her delicate way with insults . . .

Sitting there in the dark of the house, he called up the memory of the first time he had known — really known — that she loved him. They were on a picnic in the burning fields of Drezna. At first, they were very formal and polite with each other. He had been nervous to ask her out. He was just an archivist, and she was an officer in the goblin army, a lieutenant. Alone, she had once slain a rogue ogre.

"Shall I carry the picnic basket for a while, Lieutenant?"

"It's very kind of you to ask, Archivist."

In the evening, as the sky and most of the land turned red, they sat together eating cold turkey drumsticks and wearing green-shaded glasses to watch the lava burn.

He talked to her about military history, the question of strategy and tactics in past eras. She was fascinated by the stories he had to tell her of historical troop movements and flanking maneuvers. She added her own stories of modern battle. They talked about how, a thousand years before, when the goblins had lived happily in the forests and fields below the Bonecruel Mountains, they'd been defeated and swept out by the barbarian elf-king Degravaunt; Werfel and Blanchepon argued about whether the goblin army of that long-vanished time could have done something differently to achieve victory.

At the end of that picnic, watching the distant flames leap up to the sky and blank out all the stars in red flame and oily smoke, she had laid her head on his shoulder. He asked her if she was happy, and she answered that no, he was the most boring, tedious snooze of a date she had ever met.

He knew then that they would be together forever.

He reached up and put his hand gently on her hair, and whispered happily in reply that being there with her that evening was as sweet and pleasant as being repeatedly struck in the skull with a ball-peen hammer.

They chuckled, and the sky burned.

Now, sitting alone in his dark house, Werfel reached up to his shoulder — and something touched him! Her spirit?

He jolted upright.

It was just Skardebek, rubbing his cheek with her tentacles.

"You can tell I'm sad, can't you, Bekky? Can you tell?"

But she didn't seem sad. She seemed nervous. "What's wrong?"

She skittered one way and the other through the air.

Werfel stood up, dropping his skin on the floor.

"What's going on, Skardebek?"

The icthyod mewled.

And a voice out of the darkness said, "Archivist Werfel, it's time for a report."

Skardebek screeched and darted forward to bite the intruder. Werfel reached up and grabbed her tail just in time.

It was the little gray man from the secret police. He sat on the table, looking bored.

"You may remember me," he said.

Werfel was still busy trying to hold Skardebek back as she flapped and struggled. She really wanted to bite.

"My door is always open to the Ministry of Secrets," said Werfel, irritated. "But usually I would expect it to knock."

"Sorry. It was open." The man leaned back comfortably. "After I turned the knob."

"And picked the lock."

"Exactly. Tell me about the elfin visitor. We're all anxious to know. We know there was a disturbance tonight. And a few days ago. Something with the family du Burgh?"

Werfel shushed Skardebek to calm her down. She was still a little yippy. He held her in the crook of his arm. Then he whispered, "He has made some enemies."

"How?"

Werfel thought of a kind way to say it. "He does not always seem . . . appreciative of our hospitality and the richness of goblin culture. He is anxious to fulfill his duty and give his gemstone gift to the Outworlder Ghohg."

"The Outworlder has not given us any orders yet." The gray man picked a pencil out of his girdle and twirled it between his fingers. He asked bluntly: "Is Brangwain Spurge a spy?"

Werfel didn't know how to answer. The elf was a guest. It was Werfel's duty to protect him. He couldn't turn him in to the secret police. Werfel did not want to be that kind of goblin.

But on the other hand, Spurge had tricked him. Slipped out, probably not just for a stroll. Angrily, Werfel remembered the days of stiff pride and snotty silence.

"We already know," said the secret policeman. "We are just looking for you to confirm."

And Werfel wondered whether this was a trick by the secret police. He didn't know how long the gray man had been sitting in the dark. He didn't know whether the gray man had followed them to the theater. Maybe the gray man had seen Spurge sneaking around on his own, spying.

Maybe the gray man was only waiting for Werfel to say no so that he could arrest Werfel himself as a liar and a traitor.

"Archivist?" said the gray man. "I asked whether Brangwain Spurge is a spy."

Was Spurge a guest or an enemy? Was Werfel a good host or hostile?

"We need to know," said the gray man. "And you need to tell us."

Werfel opened his mouth. He said —

A light flickered in the room. Brangwain Spurge was standing by the door, holding a lantern.

"I thought I heard voices," said Spurge.

Werfel turned back to the table.

No one was there.

"Just me," said Werfel, petting Skardebek. "Me and the awful little Bekky. She's an awful girl, isn't she? Always screeching at night."

She nestled her head on his arm. He scritch-scratched the joint where her wings met her body. She purred.

Behind him, Werfel heard the secret policeman crawling for the door.

Chapter 25

From Lord Spymaster Ysoret Clivers,
Order of the Clean Hand
To His Royal Highness, the King of Elfland

Terribly sorry, Your Highness.

In the early hours of this morning, we received a transmission from the Weed. With the first picture he sent, it was clear he sneaked off and tried to get a good look at the Well of Lightning, so we were all frightfully excited. We gathered around the vision engine, waiting with our little spy hearts going pit-a-pat for each new image to come off the printing press. Finally, we thought, a glimpse at the goblin kingdom's secrets!

Terrible disappointment. Our agent got close to the lightning thing and then some monster startled him and the old Weed shriveled. Panicked. Did a runner. Barely avoided death.

Useless, I'm afraid, Your Majesty.

It's time that we moved on to our next phase of the plan, our next use for the Weed. This is the moment, Your Highness, that you might as well reveal our plan to all of the noble sneaks, eaves-droppers, braggarts, blowhards, and back-stabbers who surround your throne.

Our use for the Weed is, of course, deeper than a simple spying mission, though it's somewhat hush-hush even here around the old Order of the C.H. He's not simply a spy; he's also an assassin.

The poor blighter doesn't even know it, but that will only make him serve us better.

As you know, the gift we sent, the carved gemstone, is not simply an artifact of ye olden days. It is also a death-dealing device. Didn't used to be. It was just a pretty gemstone when they dug it up in Your Majesty's wading pool. But before we sent it, our crack team of wizards imbued it with the power, when activated, to open a hole in the world and destroy everything for a mile around it. As soon as we know it's lodged in the palace of Ghohg the Evil One, we detonate it. It sucks everything around it out of time and space and into — well, I don't know, Your Maj, because I was never frightfully good at science, but, you know, the Great Nothing or some such. Get some wizards to explain it.

Once the gemstone is taken out of its protective lead-lined box, it's ready to blow up. Drenched in alien energies. One heavy tap will detonate it. A glancing blow. A ping. A thump. But we're not taking any chances. We can trigger it, too, once it is exposed. The Weed's been told to alert us when Ghohg the Evil One receives our explosive little gift. We get the Weed's scribble, we send a signal to activate the gemstone, it opens up a hole in the world, and *thwwup!!!* — that's the sound, Your Maj, of a whirlpool that sucks things into nothingness. The goblins' leader will disappear.

Once Ghohg the Evil One is gone and his palace has been destroyed, taking a few thousand diplomats and ministers with it, the whole goblin kingdom will be thrown into confusion. As you know, General Baligant and I have made plans to take advantage of the chaos. The army of Elfland is on the march even now, and shall be at the Bonecruel Mountains within a couple of days. By the time the goblin lookouts see the army coming, it will be too late. Ghohg will be gone, and we'll sweep in to destroy the vile monsters once and for all. We will finish the work of Your Majesty's great ancestor King Degravaunt, killing most of the goblins and burning the world free of evil forever.

Within a few weeks, Your High-High, we will take the city of Tenebrion while it's in total disorder with a smoking hole of Nothing at its center. It'll be a cinch. One month from now, my king, my leader, my tennis buddy, the dark kingdom beyond the Bonecruel Mountains will be no more, and the remaining goblins will be in chains.

Millions will die in this final battle, but the army assures me we can win. And then?

Peace, Your Highness — peace in our time is a possibility.

How sweet that sounds.

You shall be remembered for your wise and pacifying ways.

And your excellent backhand tennis serve.

See you at 3:45 pronto on the courts,
    Your humble servant,

    Ysoret Clivers, Lord Spymaster
    Earl of Lunesse
    Order of the Clean Hand

Chapter 20

The next morning, as they ate their shredded wheat, Brangwain Spurge said, "Someone was here last night."

"What do you mean?"

"I heard." Spurge chewed slowly. "You did not speak out against me."

Werfel didn't know what to say. He played with his teaspoon.

Spurge said, "Thank you."

"You thanked me last night," said Werfel miserably.

"Scholars must stick together." Intensely, Spurge said, "When this is over, and the gemstone is delivered, there will be peace between our nations. I will go back to Dwelholm and I will be greeted as a hero. Those who sent me will see that I have served the elfin nation well."

Werfel thought about what waited for him once Spurge left: the fury of the du Burghs and the hidden malice of the secret police.

He said, "That will be nice for you."

Spurge held out a long knobby finger. "I want you to come visit the kingdom of the elves. I shall be your host. We shall visit archives together."

Werfel was amazed. "Really?" he said. "You will invite me to Dwelholm?"

"This gemstone is a gesture of peace between our nations. My king would not have taken such care to send it as a gift to Ghohg the Evil One if he did not wish Dwelholm and Tenebrion to shake hands and begin a new phase in our history. He is a wise and good king."

"To shake hands," mused Werfel, holding up his cereal bowl so Skardebek could slurp the extra milk. "Maybe a new dawn . . . a new day . . ."

"As a sign of goodwill," said Spurge, "I would like to show you the gemstone." He rose from his chair and began to unwind the chain from the box.

"Right now?"

"We can inspect it together. I have seen it briefly, but I would enjoy looking at it with a fellow scholar."

"Treasured guest! Yes!" Werfel rapped the table in delight. "Allow me to dress! I cannot look on this precious stone in my pajamas."

It only took Werfel two minutes of scrambling in his wardrobe to dress himself in fine robes, a scholar's hood, and fur. He came out of his bedroom clutching paper and pencils for sketching and notes.

They stood side by side at the table, and slowly, Brangwain Spurge lifted up the casket that contained the gemstone found beneath the Elf King's wading pool. He clicked at the latch with his thumbs.

Werfel held his breath.

They did not realize that in their hands they held a bomb, a force that would tear a hole in the world a mile wide.

"One moment," muttered Spurge. "The latch seems to be stuck. Must have been damaged in the fall." He picked at it with his fingernails.

"My spectacles," said Werfel, "can be used as magnifying lenses. Watch this." He took them off and rotated the lenses while Spurge fiddled with the box. "It is an invention of my own, useful for reading old manuscripts and admiring works of art painted with single bristles of a horse's mane."

By this time, Spurge had gotten the lid open and had the box turned upside down. He was knocking on the bottom, trying to get the gem to slide out onto the table.

"Careful!" said Werfel.

"Yes, yes . . ." Spurge whammed the bottom of the box one last time, and the gem jumped out.

It glittered in the air, tumbling toward the floor.

Werfel grabbed it just before it hit.

"Gosh," he sighed.

The gem was huge — larger than his hand.

He held it out to Spurge. "Isn't it beautiful?"

They both were speechless.

They laid the carved gemstone on the table in front of them and started to inspect it closely, muttering little scholarly notes to each other and passing the magnifying lenses back and forth.

"Impressive intaglio . . ." murmured Spurge, and Werfel added, "Carved right into the center of the gemstone. That's impossible."

"Most wonderful."

"Yes. Most wonderful."

The gem was a delicate red, though it picked up unexpected jags of color from the room around it, suddenly broadcasting them. Inside were carved figures: Dead warriors. Dismembered soldiers. Flights of arrows. Spears. Pikes. Severed heads. Broken limbs. Hacked-off ears.

"Where was it found, exactly?" Werfel asked.

"Under Dwelholm. The king was excavating to build a new wading pool."

"Why do you think it is of goblin make, if it was under the palace of the elves?"

"We think it must be from a thousand years ago when the forests were ruled by your people, before you yielded them up to us."

Werfel murmured, "Before they were taken from us, yes."

Spurge nodded. "Yes, before you lost them in fair battle."

"But still, why do you think this gemstone is of goblin make?"

Spurge looked a little embarrassed. "Well, there is the . . . the subject matter."

"The battle scene? Have you identified it?"

"No, but such a . . . such a violent scene must surely have

been carved by goblins. Since that is — what your people — what you like. Brutality. Bloodshed. Evil."

Werfel said, "But this — this is an elfin army cutting up goblins."

"What an interesting perspective. But it is far more likely a goblin army cutting up elves."

"I admire your scholarship, but that is an elfin army on the attack. This was carved in celebration of an elfin victory."

"What fresh and unusual ideas you have," said Spurge, "but our experts believe it was carved in celebration of a goblin massacre."

"A massacre of goblins, yes."

"No: by goblins. It's as clear as day. Though I will of course include your interesting ideas in a footnote so that —"

"This could easily be a stone carved for your King Degravaunt after he drove my ancestors out of our ancient homeland in the forests and fields below the mountains. After he sent us wandering in the wilderness. You may be giving us, as a gift, an ancient record of our defeat."

"Your victory, rather, Archivist. This is some forgotten goblin victory during the war before your race retreated into the mountains, unwilling to fight honorably."

"'Unwilling?' Esteemed guest, ha ha ha, esteemed guest!

You must admit your glorious King Degravaunt rode out of the west with his barbarian hordes bent on slaughter, and drove us out of the homes we'd lived in for centuries. Yes, we fled to the east, into the Bonecruel Mountains and out into the fire-swept Plateau of Drume, but we left because we were not prepared for a barbarian horde to attack on griffin-back."

"We are the noble race of elves — not barbarians. Never barbarians."

"A thousand years ago, you were barbarians. Nomad warriors who had tamed the griffins of the steppe. That was the only reason you won. We never knew fire could fall from the sky. We weren't ready for an elfin warlord to attack us from above without reason or mercy."

"Correction. King Degravaunt: not a 'warlord.' A hero."

"Who massacred innocent goblins."

Spurge tapped the gem irritably. "There are no such things. These severed arms are elf arms."

"Those severed heads are goblin heads."

"These severed legs are elf legs."

"Those severed ears are goblin ears."

"YOU CANNOT TELL THAT!" Spurge barked, smacking the table so hard that the gem jumped. "ELF, GOBLIN — WE ALL HAVE THE SAME EARS!"

Their attention was caught by the stone again.

After it had bumped back onto the table, the air around it shimmered, almost like the wobble of sun on a hot road.

"Did you see that?" whispered Werfel, pointing.

"Yes. I wonder . . . It seems to have some kind of force . . . or energy. . . ." Spurge knit his brows.

"Shall we hit it again?"

"Yes. Yes, for an experiment, we shall." Spurge raised his hand and, with the back of it, slapped the gift.

Once again, there was a flare of wobble.

"Curious," he said.

"Some kind of magical field," Werfel speculated.

"Let's hit it with something harder," said Spurge. He held out his hand. "Spoon?"

Werfel handed a cereal spoon to him.

Spurge tapped the stone. "Something heavier. Your staff?"

Werfel gave him the staff.

They both leaned in very close to the gem. They could see their eyes reflected in it, refracted, grown ten times, goggling back at them.

Spurge raised the staff high above his head to give the gem a mighty knock.

"Here goes," he said. And with that —

THUMP! THUMP! THUMP!

They both turned toward the door, Spurge paused with the staff raised.

"Put the gemstone away!" Werfel hissed. "Quickly!"

He sang out to the person at the door, "One second! It's lo-ocked!" They rushed to hustle the gem back into the lead-lined box.

By the time Werfel opened the front door, the gemstone was back in its casket and Spurge was sitting nearby, looking slant-wise at a wall.

"Archivist Werfel," said a soldier. "Visitor Brangwain Spurge. His Supreme Highness the Protector Ghohg, may he rule forever, requests your presence in the palace courtyard."

Chapter 27

"I must prepare!" said Spurge, astounded. He looked around, wide-eyed. "I must wash my face! I must wear a special hat!" He felt his hooded head, as if there might be a hat concealed there. "My luggage was lost in your foul lake. Do you have a hat I could borrow?"

"Absolutely, respected visitor."

"But it won't fit me. You are so much larger than I."

Werfel was confused. "I am shorter than you," he said.

"You are taller. And your head is larger."

"Sometimes people seem taller than they are," said the goblin. "Come with me."

Werfel fetched a fancy court hat and a hood lined with the white fur of the arctic serpent and loaned it to Spurge. Away from the ears of the messenger, Werfel whispered, "Don't get your hopes up too high for this first meeting. . . . The Outworlder Ghohg is very . . . unpredictable. Very strange. He is not from this world, and values other things."

Spurge was fastening a strap around his head. "He values peace, does he not?"

"He sends thousands of goblins into the mountains to build towers of glass, or into the desert to build towers of ceramic. Other times, he sends us out to knock them down. Several hundred years ago, he made our ancestors grow their hair long for three years and then cut it all off."

The elf was confused. "Surely there is some . . . secret plan. . . . Some otherworldly plan he has, beyond our understanding?"

"That's what we thought for a couple of centuries after he started ruling over us. Then we realized he really is just weird."

"But . . ."

"He's from another world. One completely unlike ours. He cares about other things."

Spurge grabbed the goblin's arm. "I will convince him of the sincerity of the elfin negotiations for peace. But first —" He gulped deeply. "Allow me to step into my chamber and quickly practice my diplomatic speech."

Werfel began to warn him, "You may find that Ghohg does not pay much attention to speeches. . . ."

But Spurge had already held up a single finger — for *Just one minute!* — and disappeared into his room. The door slammed shut behind him.

In the awkward silence that followed, Werfel heard the muttering of a spell. The elf was transmitting a message home. *Let him tell the good news of this meeting,* Werfel thought generously. *It has been far too many years since any news was good.*

The front door opened and a guard stuck his head in. "Ready to move?" asked the guard.

"Elves," said Werfel, shaking his head. "Everything's an art. Everything in life. Even getting dressed. They put on a sweater, and it's like someone painting a portrait of a duke in velvet."

Meanwhile, in the guest room, Brangwain Spurge lay, ankles crossed, eyes closed, a foot above the bed, crackling with fire, sending a message of hope across the Bonecruel Mountains.

Chapter

28

Top Secret

Transmission

Chapter 29

From Lord Spymaster Ysoret Clivers,
Order of the Clean Hand
To His Royal Highness, the King of Elfland

Your Highness,

Very thrilling. The moment has arrived. We just received this
sketch from the Weed. He must be on his way to an audience

with the Evil One. Any moment now, he'll be in the presence of Ghohg, and he'll take the gemstone out of the protective box. It's simply brimming with energies. If it doesn't ignite itself when it's tapped or passed, we can trigger it from here.

Starting now, the wizards of the Order of the Clean Hand are going to send out the trigger signal every five minutes. The first time one of those signals hits the stone when it's exposed out of that box, it will detonate and take half the palace of Tenebrion along with it. *Foop* — and gone.

Within the hour, Your Highness, Ghohg the Evil One will be no more.

Count on it, or you can remove any one of the fingers on my own clean hands.

Your humble servant,

Ysoret Clivers, Lord Spymaster
Earl of Lunesse
Order of the Clean Hand

PS. It is a shame that we will have to lose the Weed, but I fear there really is no way to warn him. He's likely to be caught in the blast. The good news is that when he detonates, he shall probably take a few thousand of those filthy goblins with him. Shall we have him named a national hero after his tragic death? I see a statue of him mounted on a flying barrel. Sculptors can do wonderful things, making people a tad more handsome and muscly.

Chapter 30

As they walked through the crowded streets of Tenebrion, Spurge clutched the stone's box close to his chest and wrapped both arms around it.

"I should have practiced my prepared speech again," he muttered to Werfel.

"There will be time," Werfel replied.

Werfel's neighbor called out to him, "On your way to embarrass yourself at court, you dismal little toad?"

Werfel waved cheerfully. "Anything to put a mile between you and me, Druzmilla."

He shooed Skardebek back to the house. The little icthyod

seemed anxious, worried. Werfel kissed her and then snapped his fingers and pointed at the house. She flapped back into an upstairs window, mewling unhappily.

The two scholars climbed up through the levels of the city, the guards marching behind them.

As they passed through the huge palace gates, Werfel warned Spurge, "You should be prepared to dance."

"Dance? Dance how?"

"The Outworlder Ghohg likes people to dance around him."

"We'll wait outside for you, Archivist," said one of the guards. "Good luck."

"Not coming in?"

The guard shrugged. "I can't dance."

"What is this?" said Spurge, confused.

He and Werfel walked into the courtyard of the palace.

Probably a thousand goblins, courtiers and diplomats and civil servants, were spread out around the courtyard, and all of them were dancing in strict rhythm in a great spiral. They extended their legs and stepped one way, then the other. They each spun in place, a thousand at once, and then continued to tread the stately spiral. On towers all around the courtyard, bands of musicians played a vast, slow tune on quacking horns, blaring trumpets, and thundering drums, while below, the spiral moved to their beat.

At the center was a raised dais, and on that dais, towering above the dancing politicians, stood Ghohg.

Spurge gasped. "It is him. I have seen him on posters, but..."

"Drawings cannot capture his strange majesty."

"Or whether he is right side up. Are those wings or claws?"

"I cannot even see what you mean. Dance. Just dance. Quickly, guest. Join the dance."

Stiffly, Spurge tried to follow the motions of the courtiers around him. As he spun, he asked, "What are we doing?"

"He likes everyone dancing around him like the whirling of suns and galaxies. People will be moved slowly to the center, and then they can present their petitions or state their cases. Some people will be forced to spiral in, and some people will be forced to spiral out. But if you don't dance in time — quick! and a left, and a right, and a left, left, right — then you'll never be called up. You'll be told to leave in disgrace."

Spurge was not the only emissary from another land. There were humans there, and dwarves, and even a few of the unutterable creatures from the strange lands to the north, all of them waiting on the great Ghohg, hoping he would grace them with his otherworldly attentions. They danced, too, bowing and turning in the solemn spiral.

An official with a clipboard danced up to them. "Name and purpose?" he said.

"I am Magister Brangwain Spurge, emissary from the kingdom of Elfland, and I bring a gift of great price to Ghohg the Evil One, as a peace offering in hopes —"

"Thank you, yes." The goblin scribbled on his pad while Werfel coaxed Spurge under his breath, "Quick — and a slide left, tap tap with the right, and a kick and two and three and a . . ."

"Should I take the stone out of the box?" Spurge asked the official. "I could hold it up. Does he wish to see it?"

"Not necessary, but up to you," said the goblin, checking his clipboard. "If he doesn't call you up to the throne today, then come back tomorrow or next Monday. We may send out someone with more questions to — Hey, watch your step, sir! These are soft-toed slippers I'm wearing. That's right. Glissade right and do-si-do your partner."

The official joined another column of courtiers dancing in the opposite direction and soon disappeared from sight. Werfel bowed to noblemen and noblewomen who passed.

"Does the court dance around the Evil One like this every day?"

"My esteemed guest might do well to stop calling our ruler 'the Evil One' before we reach him."

"Is this what happens in the palace every day?"

"No. Only on certain days. Other times, the orders come out of a slit in the door."

"I wish to catch his attention. I think I shall open the box and hold up the gemstone so it will sparkle as we dance around him."

Werfel agreed. "That is actually the kind of gesture that might catch the eye of Ghohg, Protector of the People. Though it is unclear to us whether the Outworlder has eyes."

As they danced in the circle and music played, Spurge lifted the metal box hanging around his neck so he could expose the gemstone to the sun.

He did not know that trigger pulses were being sent through the air from across the Bonecruel Mountains. He had no idea that he was about to blast open a huge, gaping hole that would swallow him and everything around him.

He fumbled with the catch. "Once again, it is stuck."

"Perhaps my honorable colleague will allow me to try?"

"It does not feel right that anyone but me should open the box in the presence of your dark and gruesome king."

"Of course, my guest knows best."

"Aha! Now I think I've got it!"

The latch popped.

Inside the box, the stone wriggled with magical energies.

Spurge prepared to lift the lid off with his thumbs. "Let the light of this ancient gem, so long separated from its goblin makers —"

"Could be elfin makers," Werfel pointed out.

"So long separated from its *goblin* makers now shine out in peace, in glittering joy, over the courtyard of —"

Werfel urged, "The dance, elfin visitor!"

"I am trying to open this box with a little ceremony."

"As you should. But don't forget to dance or we shall be thrown out of the Great Protector's presence! Left, left, right. And hop! Hop!"

Doggedly, Spurge jumped up and down, jolting the stone.

It quivered in its casket.

"May I continue?" Spurge asked.

"Please, treasured visitor."

So Spurge took a huge breath, held the box above his head, prepared to flip open the lid, and declared, "Let the light of this ancient gem, so long separated from its goblin makers, now shine out in peace, in glittering joy, over the courtyard of —"

Spurge didn't finish his sentence. Werfel looked at the scholar to see what was wrong.

Spurge's eyes were huge. He was watching a group of soldiers with a trained vork in a metal collar.

"Ah," said Werfel, "that is a vork. Very fierce. We have domesticated them, however, so they serve us. Magister Spurge, why do you appear so worried? Is it —"

And then the creature looked straight at Spurge and screamed bloody murder.

Chapter

31

Top Secret
Transmission

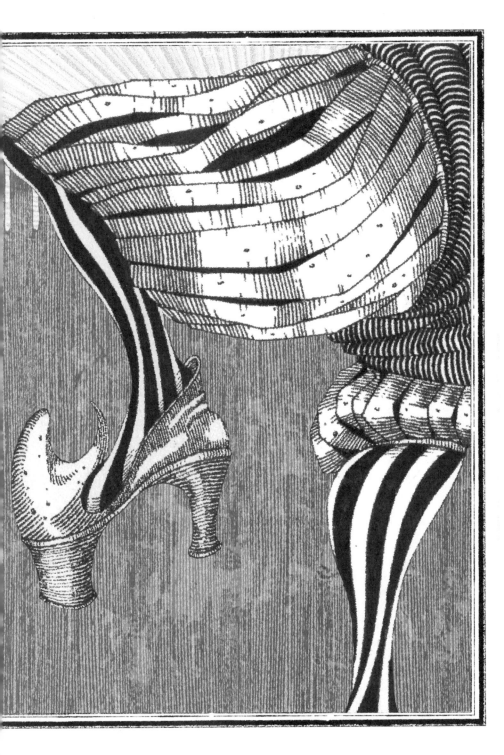

Chapter 32

Courtiers were pouring over the cobblestones, screaming and shoving. Soldiers ran forward with pikes and swords,
shouting commands and questions to one another. In the center, Ghohg burned with a furious light.

Spurge and Werfel tripped and dodged through the terrified crowd. Werfel had no idea what was going on. It was clear
the vork recognized Spurge—and that for some reason,
Spurge recognized the vork. Above the mob, soldiers were

trying to figure out who in the fleeing crowd had caught the monster's eye.

Werfel was confused and furious. Somehow, he knew the elf had betrayed him and that now, as a result, they both were in mortal danger. In that moment, Werfel hated Brangwain Spurge.

At the same time, he knew it made sense to run. Everyone was running. "I don't know what you did, esteemed guest," Werfel said in Elven, "but if those soldiers see you, we are in trouble."

At the soonest possible moment, he pulled Spurge into a doorway and said, "We have to hide your face. Take off that stupid hat!" He batted at the ceremonial hat. It was buttoned around the elf's neck. In rage, Werfel popped the button and threw the hat to the floor. Spurge shied away from Werfel's rage, but Werfel seized his shoulder and pulled the white fur hood down further so it covered the elf's face.

"Now — keep your head low. Walk like a goblin. We have to get back through the city without anyone noticing us." He shook Spurge. "Guest — I do not think they saw that it was you."

They rejoined the fleeing crowds.

Then the mob stopped flowing. Werfel hopped up like a toad to see what the holdup was. "Oh, no," he said. "The guards are checking everyone at the gate."

A voice called out through a megaphone: "Please remain calm! The vork has recognized one of you! One of you attempted to break into the Well of Lightning yesterday. Stop crowding, people. Let the vork stare. Put your hands down. Each of you must be sniffed by the vork."

"Oh, dear," said Spurge.

Werfel shot the elf a dirty glance. Then he mumbled, "Follow me, Magister. There's a garden over here with a low wall." He led the way through the throng.

Behind them, the voice over the megaphone called out, "If you have any other crimes you would like to confess to the Ministry of Silence, this would be a good time to do that."

The two scrambled to the garden. It had a wide terrace overlooking the goblin city. Werfel led the elf behind some bushes, and they climbed down a brick wall. They were out of the palace.

They walked down through the levels of the city as if nothing was wrong, as if nothing interesting was happening. Werfel was very careful to walk at a normal speed, though his heart was racing, and everything in his body and brain was complaining about disaster.

No one noticed the elf's features, because they were hidden by the hood. Unfortunately, they did notice the large, fancy metal box hung around his neck with a chain. It clanked at every step. People turned to look.

"Take the gem out," said Werfel. "I'll hide it under my robe. We'll throw the box away. You don't need the box."

"I have . . . I have been given a sacred task by the Elf King. I will not . . ."

Werfel looked grim, but he didn't argue. He just said, "If anyone from the Ministry of Secrets asks, we just have to tell them that yes, we were in the crowd, but we fled like everyone else when the vork went on the rampage. They'll never know it recognized you."

"You don't think they figured it out?"

"I hope not, esteemed guest," said Werfel. "Because otherwise, both you and I are dead."

They were back in Werfel's neighborhood. It was quiet. People were at work or school. The two tried to walk casually through the streets.

Until they came to the corner near Werfel's house.

Werfel reached out his arm and slammed Spurge to the side. Spurge tumbled into an alley.

"Ow!" Spurge complained. "You hit the chain!"

Werfel said, "My house is surrounded by soldiers. Eight or nine. On the lookout. They're waiting for us to come back. They know it was you. Whatever it was you did." Werfel couldn't control his temper anymore, so he stopped talking. What he was thinking was: *However you betrayed me, Magister Spurge. However you sneaked out of that theater and spied and made me a liar to the secret police.*

And then he realized: *Skardebek! Skardebek is still in the house. What if I never see her again? My little Bekky . . .*

Werfel rocked from foot to foot. It was the closest he could come to pacing in the cramped space. "What are we going to do?" he said. "If they catch us, you're going to be put to death as a spy and I'm going to be tortured and put to death for helping you. You were my responsibility. We have to get away. Somehow. Somehow."

"You have to get away?" a sharp, gravelly voice said in the darkness. "You think you can get away, you traitorous little toad?"

Chapter 33

Werfel looked up in shock. A shambling form loomed in the shadows of the alley.

Brangwain Spurge backed away, shivering. He clutched the metal box to him, as if he still could protect it, or as if it could somehow protect him.

"You will . . . you will not take me alive," he croaked. "I have done nothing wrong."

"Hmm," said the voice at the end of the alley. "Skittish

one, isn't he? What dungheap have you fallen into this time, Archivist?"

"I'm afraid I don't have time for friendly insults," said Werfel. "Magister Spurge, you remember my neighbor Druzmilla. Madam, the secret police have surrounded my house and wish to arrest us."

She came into the light. "I saw. What have you gotten yourself into, you wretched sop?"

"I don't even know," said Werfel. "But you have to help us get out of the city before we're arrested. Please, Druzmilla."

"Why would she help us?" Spurge protested. "I'm an elf! She'll give us up quick as crickets!"

Werfel drew himself up. "She'll help us because we all help each other when it comes to the secret police. No one likes them. And she'll help us, Magister Spurge, because she is a dear friend. And my friends — my actual friends — do not betray me." He stared hard into Brangwain Spurge's guilty, uncomfortable eyes.

They heard the rhythmic clank of armor on the street. More soldiers were arriving at Werfel's house. Werfel heard the voice of the agent from the secret police calling out, "Make sure the back door to the house is covered, too. And spread out through the streets and alleys. They must be here somewhere."

Spurge closed his eyes and held his breath in panic.

"This way," said Druzmilla, opening the door into her kitchen.

They rushed through her house. There were children everywhere, sitting under chairs and on tables. As the two scholars ran past the wondering kids, Druzmilla announced, "You see nothing, children. This is just the wind blowing doors open and closed again. There is nothing in front of your eyes."

She peered out the door into her little courtyard. When she was sure the coast was clear, she beckoned to Werfel and Spurge.

"Get into the donkey cart," she said. "Lie down. I'll hitch up the donkey. And I'll find something to put on top of you to hide you."

Spurge and Werfel clambered into the cart. There was a balled-up tarpaulin in it. Werfel spread out the tarp and Spurge pulled it over himself. Werfel tried to get under it, too. Half of Werfel still stuck out. He pulled it a little toward him.

Now half of Spurge stuck out. Spurge pulled it his way.

Now half of Werfel stuck out.

Werfel sighed. "Honored guest," he said wearily.

"No, no," said Spurge, ashamed. "You take the tarp. I will be exposed."

"No. I am your host. Allow me to tuck you into the tarp, as I would make your bed with white sheets of the finest Dunobrian silk."

"No, you have been too kind. Take the tarp and —"

"Shut up, both of you," said Druzmilla. "Here come rubber inner tubes."

She dumped a load of old inner tubes on top of them. The smell of burnt rubber was overwhelming. Spurge retched.

The tarp didn't cover Werfel's eyes or the tips of Spurge's toes.

"That's not enough," said Druzmilla. "I don't have anything else to cover you." She thought for a moment. "Aha."

They heard her go to the door.

"Children!" she shouted. "Picnic!"

She perched children on top of the goblin, the elf, and the inner tubes. She plastered the whole cart with her kids.

"Little Jax," mumbled Werfel, "if you sit on Uncle Werfel's mouth and nose, I won't be able to breathe and I will die."

But Druzmilla was yipping to the donkey, and they were rolling out of the courtyard.

"Stay low," she said. "There are guards and secret police everywhere."

The kids jounced around on top of them, bickering and shoving one another, pretending they were just going for a ride in a pile of junk.

Werfel could feel the wheels bump across the cobblestones. He could see the blue sky and the gutters roll by up above. They must be on the street now. They must be in front of Druzmilla's house. Now they must be in front of his own house. Right near the line of guards. This was the most dangerous moment. He held his breath.

And at that moment, he heard a familiar squeal and screech.

Skardebek. She had flown out a window. She must have smelled him. She was fluttering around Druzmilla's head. The kids all screamed with delight.

Werfel could hear guards wandering over to see what all the ruckus was.

Normally, Druzmilla would have greeted Skardebek lovingly, maybe griping that someone had just picked a big scab and thrown it out the window, but she was clearly too nervous to think of a pleasant insult. The little icthyod was hovering around, chirping and sniffing Werfel.

Through the gaps in rubber inner tubes and children, Werfel saw his beloved Skardebek darting down toward him, her little black eyes fixed on his eyes. She was waiting for him to jump up and embrace her.

His beloved little girl was about to give him away.

"What's that?" said a guard. "That his pet?"

"It's his pet," said another one.

"He must be around."

"Lady — what's in the cart? Under the kids?"

Druzmilla said, "We're collecting garbage." She jumped down with the largest children, and they all started forking garbage from a heap into the cart, right on top of the inner tubes, Werfel, and Spurge. It smelled terrible. Coffee grounds, chicken skin, bat guano, and some kind of old fat.

As Werfel's eyes disappeared under fish skulls, Skardebek squealed in annoyance. Druzmilla added, "Yeah. That little pustule loves the taste of trash. That's what she's after. Snacks." The icthyod was burrowing downward through the slime. Finding Werfel's face to lick.

"If you see the Archivist, you tell us!" the guard said.

"Sure thing," Druzmilla agreed. "Back on the heap, kids!" They all climbed aboard. Druzmilla clicked to the donkey so he walked on.

Skardebek had found Werfel's nose and was licking it joyfully. She snuggled close to his cheek and purred.

They rolled down the street away from the only home he had ever known.

The cart bounced and jounced over the dirt streets and cobblestones. Werfel guessed they were at the edge of his neighborhood. He could hear the clanging of the tinsmiths and the coppersmiths. Then that faded, too. Werfel figured it would take another hour or so to get out of the city.

The Archivist squirmed under the kids and garbage. He was

incredibly uncomfortable. Next to him, Spurge was trying to lie as still as possible, but he still kicked Werfel in the side with his knee whenever they went over a bump.

There were a lot of bumps.

They passed through a crowd — maybe the large market on Groffnith Avenue. Merchants sang out the names of what they sold. "Oysters! Pickled oysters! Large pickled oysters!" "Hams and steaks! Of all manner of beast! Rump and round!" "Paper! Finest paper! Write to your love, write to your nanna! Let them know you care!"

Then the noise died down. They were on some backstreet. No sound but the squeaking of the wheels on the cart and the fighting of two kids on Werfel's gut.

And then a great sniffing.

A loud sniffing.

Skardebek quivered next to Werfel's head, as if she could tell something was wrong.

Werfel heard Druzmilla warn him beneath her breath, "Archivist . . . game is up. There's a vork headed this way with its snout to the ground. It must smell elf. Get ready to run."

The sniffing got louder.

And Druzmilla shouted dramatically, "What is that? Who's in my garbage heap? What? Who? Get out! Out! Help!"

Werfel grabbed Spurge by the skinny wrist and yanked him

up out of the trash. They had to make sure that it looked like they had stowed away on Druzmilla's cart without her knowledge. Otherwise she and her children could be imprisoned, too.

"Filthy woman!" Werfel yelled, and he and Spurge hopped out of the cart — narrowly avoiding the huge swinging beak of the vork, which carked like a monstrous crow.

"Help me, guards!" cried Druzmilla in fake distress. "Help my little wee ones! Oh, ack and alas, the poor children!"

Spurge and Werfel stumbled backward, shocked to see so many guards staring at them.

And then they saw a huge monster of a man in armor standing next to the vork. Someone who had apparently volunteered to help search. Someone who was staring at them with a sneer and hatred.

Regibald du Burgh.

Chapter

34

Top Secret
Transmission

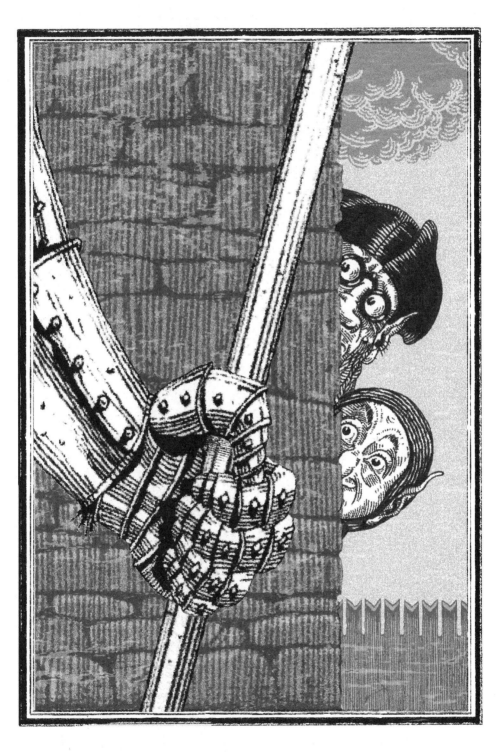

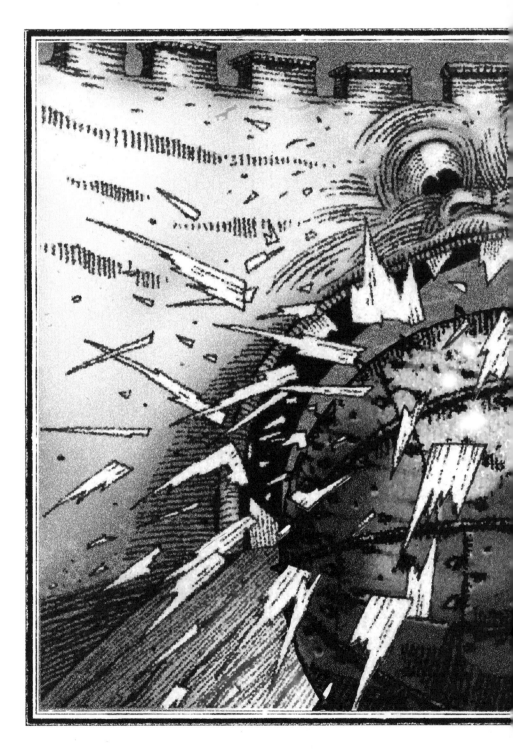

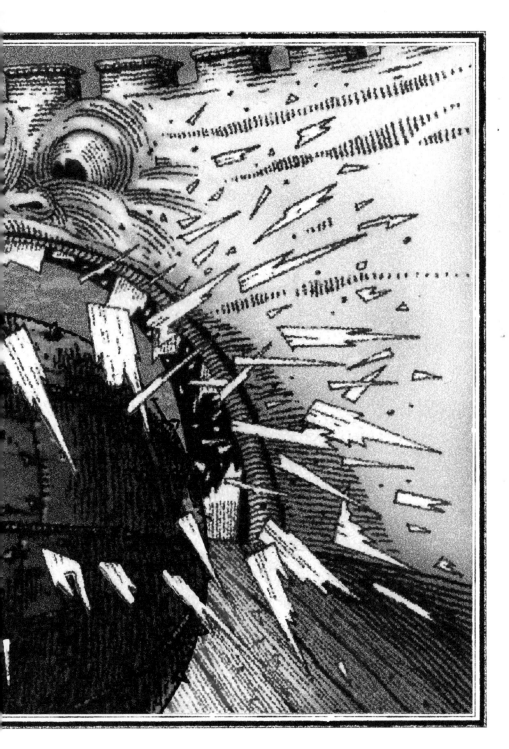

Chapter 35

From Lord Spymaster Ysoret Clivers,
Order of the Clean Hand
To His Royal Highness, the King of Elfland

Your Majesty,

How delightful to see Your Majesty in your audience chamber earlier. As I informed Your Majesty, it appears we have suffered a temporary delay. Your Majesty asked to see the latest sendings from the Weed, and I enclose them;

perhaps you can make more sense of them than I can. We cannot determine exactly what went wrong, but it is sadly clear that Spurge has left the city of Tenebrion, apparently without delivering the gemstone to the Evil One. This is not the outcome we wished for. Of course, you have my deepest apologies for this error, and I assure you we are doing what we can to fix it.

On another matter, which is perhaps of less national interest but of great personal interest to me in particular: I must protest, Your Highness, that I did not really expect you to take me quite seriously when I offered one of my fingers in exchange for failure. When your bodyguard and champion showed up at my office, I was expecting something more in the way of an invitation to play tennis. Instead, he spread my hand out on my desk and, taking out his ax —

Well, really, Your Majesty.

And if I may be allowed to speak plainly, I think, given our long friendship, you might have allowed me to at least select the finger. The pinkie is hardly ever used; whereas I often use the index finger when I want to make an important point. Now what do I do? Gesture with the whole hand like a fish merchant?

On top of that, I am in quite a bit of pain.

Nonetheless, I wish to state in the strongest of terms that

I am still your loyal servant, and that the Order of the Clean Hand shall still bring everything to a satisfactory conclusion, though we might be down one finger.

At the moment, General Baligant has sent me an unkind note. His army is still on the march toward the kingdom of the goblins, and yet Ghohg has not been destroyed as promised. The army will halt their march when we can get word to them; otherwise, they would be walking willingly into the armed teeth of the goblin kingdom. We are coming up with an alternative plan, if Your Majesty will give us just a short time to do so.

Our spies among your loyal subjects tell us that only very few want another war, and that word is starting to leak out that the army is on the march right toward the goblins. We are worried there might be protests here in Dwelholm. As a result, we at the Order have taken the liberty of rounding up all the bards, singers, preachers, and printers who might complain, and we've slapped them in prison.

The glory of elfdom shall not be dimmed by the whining of a few crybabies.

We shall be victorious — we shall find a way to destroy Ghohg and to reduce the goblins to slavery, as we did the dwarves of the Vushnigar Deeps, who toil to make your court such delightful gold trinkets. In a year, the goblins will be forced to work in our mines, and you will regret ever having removed the index finger from

Your servant and eternal friend,

Ysoret Clivers, Lord Spymaster
Earl of Lunesse
Order of the Clean Hand

Chapter 36

The vast plain was hairy with dead grasses. Two tiny figures made their way through the center of it: Magister Brangwain Spurge and the goblin archivist Werfel, fleeing from the crashed sphere. They avoided the stone farmhouses on rock outcroppings by walking in irrigation ditches. The sun burned brightly above them.

Suddenly, Spurge looked around wildly and clutched at his chest. "Archivist!" he croaked. "Archivist, I have lost the gemstone! I must have left the box in that woman's donkey cart!"

"There's nothing you can do about it now."

"It is priceless! A gift from the Elf King!"

"Lost now, esteemed guest."

"No! We must go back into the city. Right now. We must go back and find it. I must defend it with my life."

Werfel started walking toward the distant mountains.

"Where are you going?" asked Spurge.

"Away from the city."

"I said we need to return to the city."

"Going back there right now is a death sentence, Magister Spurge. It would not be heroic. You will be caught, imprisoned, and tortured. So we are going away from the city."

"Archivist!" Spurge whined.

"We are going this way," said Werfel. "We are going to lose ourselves in the mountains before we're found and thrown in a dungeon or killed."

For a while, Spurge argued, but Werfel kept trekking across dry pastures, and Spurge kept following him, pleading, until the city of Tenebrion was just a distant dot behind them on the horizon.

It was late in the day, and the sun was going down on the Plateau of Drume. The two scholars were trudging between boulders.

Spurge had the good sense to keep quiet. He sometimes looked sheepishly at his goblin host.

Werfel was furious and anxious. He had no idea what they should do next. He was just trying to get them away from the prying eyes of guards and farmers.

All day, as they walked, he pictured what was going on back at his house. The guards and the secret police would be searching each room. When the secret police conducted raids, they always made a point of tearing things up, ruining furniture, wrecking stuff. They didn't care what they found.

Werfel had spent years collecting little historical artifacts like castles carved out of ogre tusks, copper coins from the Six Kingdoms period, and dainty little paintings of goblins in love, leaning over walls or strumming on the lute, painted by the court artists of five hundred years before. He was proud of every item in his collection. He had chosen each one so carefully over the years. But they would all be destroyed, defaced, trampled underfoot. The secret police hated beautiful things.

Even worse, Werfel had collected some of the airy art of elfinkind, captured generations ago in some raid — paintings of heroes riding griffins and kings playing chess. He had just hung them on the guest room walls. They would be used against him. The secret police would report that he was not just a scholar of elf-goblin relations — he was a secret agent of the elves, a traitor against his own people.

He was no traitor. On this afternoon, trekking across the bleak Plateau of Drume, he hated elves with a passion.

He would never see his home again, never step inside that

door off the street he loved, where Druzmilla's many kids screamed and slid down the railings. He and Skardebek would never snuggle by the fire on cold, rainy nights.

Skardebek didn't understand the disaster that had befallen them. She was calmer now, resting on his shoulder, licking her tentacles to clean them.

The sun was setting behind the Bonecruel Mountains. Spurge and Werfel were crossing a crater where some ancient battle must have happened. Skeletons were scattered among the rocks. Skulls in helmets stuck out of the dirt. A rib cage caught the last light of evening.

Faintly, Brangwain Spurge asked, "What will we do for dinner?"

Werfel stopped walking and stared at the elf in fury. "I don't know," he said. "How do you expect me to know?"

"I was just asking. The sun is going down."

"Allow me to point out, valued guest, that if we are being followed by the army, they are probably using guide-vork, which do not need daylight to sniff us out. And we are also being followed, no doubt, by Regibald du Burgh, who will stop at nothing to kill us. So as your host, I recommend we keep hiking into the night." He started walking again, his footsteps scrunching on gravel, stones, and bone.

Brangwain Spurge sniffed. "Awful place, this plateau." When

he got no answer, he added, "Bleak. Nothing here. Nothing but death." Werfel still didn't say anything, so Spurge said, "I was surprised to see farms. Can't believe anything would grow here." This didn't get any answer, either, so he said, "The fields and orchards around Dwelholm are beautiful at this time of year." He sighed. "If I were home, the corn would be ripe, and the apples would be starting to grow on the trees. The wheat fields would be golden." He pointed off into the distance, where houses were clinging to the far wall of a crater. Their little lights burned. "I don't know why anyone would try to live in a place like this," Spurge said.

Werfel turned on him. "Don't you? Don't you know? *Don't you know why we live in a place like this?*" Suddenly, he couldn't control himself anymore.

All the days of anger and resentment boiled up in him. He was tired of being nice. Tired of trying to be a generous host. Tired of being walked all over. He shouted, "How DARE you talk about the beautiful orchards around Dwelholm right now! How DARE you! All the apples! All the corn! All the wheat! *Why do we live here? Because we were forced out of those orchards by you! By elves! Your people attacked us without warning, killed us, and left us to flee into the mountains!*" He was bellowing into the elf's pale face. "YOU WALK AROUND LIKE SOME SUPERIOR SPECIES, BUT YOU'RE NO BETTER THAN WE ARE!"

"There is no need, Archivist Werfel, to take that tone with me."

"Isn't there? ISN'T THERE? You have cost me my job, my home, my friends, and, if we're not careful, my life. I have done nothing but try to please you for almost a week, and you have complained. You have sneered. You have stuck your nose in the air. You have called us names. You have sent home reports — oh, I know about that — and who knows what they say? Who knows if they're even true? You have endangered me. You have endangered yourself. IN SHORT, MY VALUED GUEST, YOU ARE A COMPLETE —" and here he started swearing.

Werfel's voice echoed around the rocks and stones and cliffs, over the skeletons of the fallen dead.

That was too bad, because something hiding far up on the rocks heard the shouting and stirred in its cave.

Down below, Spurge protested, "I am here on behalf of the king of Elfland! Bringing a gift of peace!"

"A gift of peace? A GIFT OF PEACE? You brought us a stone showing the defeat of our people by murderous elves, by your crazy, bloodthirsty, cruel, barbarian King Degravaunt —"

"Actually, a massacre by goblins."

"AND YOU EXPECT US TO WELCOME YOU WITH

OPEN ARMS? SO YOUR PEOPLE CAN ATTACK US AGAIN?"

"Now, that is not fair! That is not fair, Archivist! My people are a peace-loving people and would never attack the kingdom of the goblins if they weren't attacked first!"

Werfel drew in a big breath so he could start yelling again. But he didn't yell. His mouth stayed flapped open.

A huge shadow was growing above Spurge's head. Something gigantic was rising up. It blocked out the early stars.

"And another thing," said Spurge, but Werfel screamed, "RUN!"

The towering figure roared: a creature so large that a man could have bathed in the soupy spittle of its mouth and sat curled up in the chambers of its heart. More eyes kept appearing in its head.

The scholars dashed hectically across the sand, leaping over the bones of previous victims. A giant hand reached down to grab the goblin archivist. Werfel scrabbled in the dirt and pulled out an old, rusted sword — but it was only a snapped-off hilt. Still, he waved it in the air menacingly. "You'll never eat us!" he shrieked, and, steeling himself, ran toward the ogre's knee.

The ogre watched him in surprise.

Werfel swung the ancient hilt.

It was totally rusted. It hit the ogre and broke in two.

The ogre's many eyes blinked in chorus. It licked its lips and reached out for the panicked goblin. Werfel stumbled, keeping the elf behind him.

There was no place for them to run. They were backed against a rock wall, knee-deep in a long-dead soldier.

The creature leaned closer, filling the air with its venomous breath.

Werfel clenched his hands and started to say a prayer to Great Rugwith.

"Kind host," whispered Spurge, "I have an idea."

Chapter

38

Top Secret
Transmission

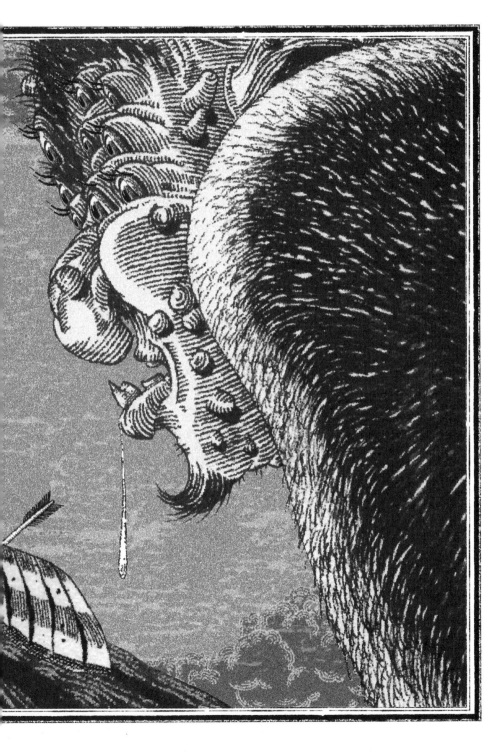

Chapter 39

The morning after their escape from the ogre, Spurge and Werfel both woke up hungry and irritable. Skardebek had found something dead and rotten to eat, so she was chirpy. The two scholars, however, were not.

Werfel sat on a flat stone, looking at the rising sun. He was thinking about what Blanchepon, his beloved Blanchepon, would have told him to do if she were still alive. She would have helped them survive in the wild.

But no, he realized. She would hate him now, because he had betrayed his own people, his own city, by helping the elf.

After he sat that way without moving for a long time,

he picked up two pebbles and rolled them from one hand to the other. He listened to the plink they made when they collided.

Behind him, Spurge said, "I am going to send a signal to the Order of the Clean Hand. I am going to ask them to pick me up."

"Do whatever you wish, esteemed guest," said Werfel bitterly.

"I need to tell them where to find me. We need a meeting spot."

"They're not going to pick you up."

"Is there a place you know where we could hide until the griffin-riders come for me? Someplace in the Bonecruel Mountains? Someplace with a landmark they could recognize from the air?"

Werfel thought it over. "On the far side of the mountains, facing Elfland, there is one of Ghohg's glass towers. It is shattered, but the ruins still stand. They could see it from the air. If they actually came for you."

Nervously, Spurge said, "Will you draw me a map?"

Angrily, Werfel stirred himself. He got out a stick and drew a map in the dirt.

Spurge studied it for several minutes and nodded. "I will go do the magical spell of communication now. I will contact the Order."

Werfel nodded, looking at the baking sun as it rose higher.

Spurge said, "Lord Clivers promised. They will extract me."

Werfel muttered, "Like a bad tooth."

The elf started to walk away but then stopped. He admitted, "I failed, you know."

Werfel turned around to look at him.

"I know," said Werfel. "You lost the stupid gemstone."

"No. I was a failure as a spy. When I sneaked away from the opera. I was supposed to figure out how the Well of Lightning worked. But I am a scholar, not a secret agent. I got frightened. That vork smelled me and almost killed me. It chased me away. I didn't see anything. I didn't send anything of use to my people."

Werfel felt like he should say something nice so that Spurge would feel better about himself, but that didn't really make sense, seeing as the elf had been trying to spy on Werfel's people.

Spurge said, "I failed my king."

"I failed my city," Werfel said. "I should have turned you in."

Spurge twitched uncomfortably.

But it was Spurge who said, "Archivist Werfel, I am sorry."

Werfel shaded his eyes and looked at the scrawny elf.

Spurge repeated, "I am sorry. I am sorry I abused your hospitality. And got you involved in my spying. And forced you to flee with me here."

"I can't go back," said Werfel. "I can never go back."

"I'm sorry."

Werfel asked, "How can that be enough? An apology? It's nothing but air. Air weighs nothing." He shook his head. He threw his two pebbles off into the plain and said, "You know that your griffin-riders won't come to get you, right?"

"Of course they will. For this mission, I am an employee of the Order of the Clean Hand, our secret police. They are very powerful. They're the ones who asked me to come here."

"That's exactly why they won't come to save you," said Werfel.

"I am sorry you think so." Spurge sniffed. He looked out at the horizon. To make conversation, he said, "At least it's a beautiful sunrise, Archivist."

"It's not a beautiful sunrise," said Werfel, turning away. "It's too red. That means we may have firestorms soon. We need to get out of the foothills and into the mountains as soon as possible."

Werfel didn't turn back around, but he heard Spurge slink away.

In a few minutes, Werfel saw the glow from the crackling lightning flicker on the rocks as the elf meditated and hovered in the air.

He shook his head and closed his eyes.

The demon sun got higher, hotter, and brighter in the sky.

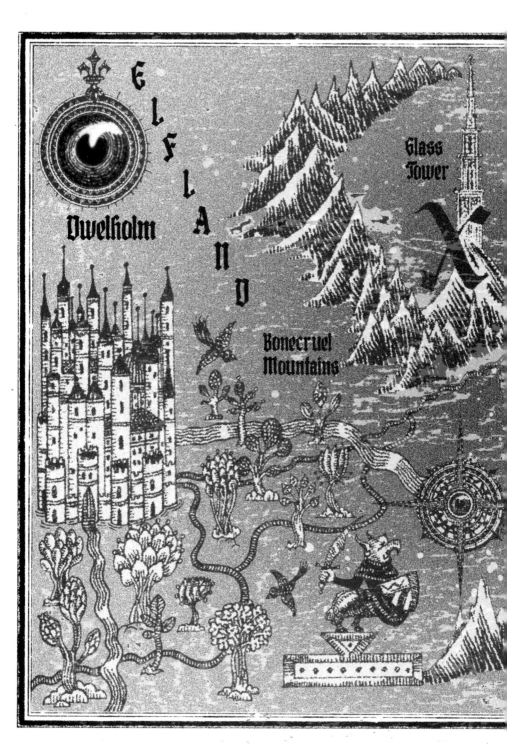

KINGDOM OF GOBLINS

Tenebrion

Plateau of Drume

Chapter 40

From Lord Spymaster Ysoret Clivers,
Order of the Clean Hand
To His Royal Highness, the King of Elfland

Your Majesty,

We have just received a message directly from the court of Ghohg the Evil One addressed to your excellent self. It requests a meeting between you and Ghohg at the border between our kingdoms. He says he wishes you to "dance with him," a request that I must admit has me a little bit puzzled, though from the Weed's images of Ghohg's palace, there does seem to be a lot of dancing.

General Baligant's army is already most of the way to the border, cooling their heels and dusting their epaulets while they wait for your orders. We could all go out and join them, and you could parley with Ghohg if that tickled your fancy. I suspect that it has something to do with the Weed's cover being blown. They know we sent a spy into their kingdom. This could be dangerous. Your Maj, they may want to start a war.

We continue to receive messages from the Weed, poor thing. There is no explanation of what happened to the gemstone. It has simply disappeared from his pictures. He just sent us an X-marks-the-spot map on how to find him, should we want to extract him. Of course, there's no question of us rescuing him at this point. The government of Elfland must deny everything to do with him.

If we did fetch him, it would be an admission of guilt — that he really was an assassin working for us. It would cause an international incident. A diplomatic disaster. The goblins would go to war against us again.

On the other hand, if we do nothing and let the poor Weed dangle, he will just disappear, killed in some ravine or mountain pass, and we can pretend we didn't know anything about his mission, and that he didn't have any mission other than delivering that moldy old stone. We can claim that he was just a nincompoop or a madman.

I do wish we didn't have to abandon him. It really is rather rusty for the old Weed, who did not know he was being sent as an assassin. But there is no help for it.

Do tell me how you want us to respond to the invitation from Ghohg the Evil One. If we're setting out for the border, we should do so at once.

Pack your dancing shoes.

Your faithful servant,

Ysoret Clivers, Lord Spymaster
Earl of Lunesse
Order of the Clean Hand

Chapter 41

Hunger and heat.

The plain blistered beneath the sun. The two scholars had not eaten for more than a day.

And as they both realized, they were not good at survival in the wild. They had been trained to live in libraries and museums.

They crossed over rocky dunes of burnt old grass. In the distance, the Bonecruel Mountains rose up, green with pines but so far away.

Around noon, there were no shadows. Werfel and Spurge found a pond to drink from, with a few trees around it.

They waded in the water, slurping desperately.

Werfel said, "I wish we had a canteen to carry some of this water."

"How much longer until we're up in the mountains?"

"Probably tomorrow. Drink up, little Bekky. Drink up, my squishy little girl." Werfel dunked himself and soaked his beard.

He climbed out onto the bank and sat for a minute with his back against a tree. "Aha," he said. "Look, esteemed guest. Gorgonbladder." He began to pull a plant out of the ground. "We can eat this."

"I do hate to disagree with my goblin colleague, but that's called cloudflower. And it's deathly poisonous."

"It's gorgonbladder. And our soldiers dig it up and eat it when they're starving."

"If you eat it, you will fall over backward and die."

"You are mistaken."

"I have read many books of herbal lore."

"So have I. And I can tell you the roots are edible."

"The flowers are — oh. The roots." Spurge looked embarrassed and crossed his arms. "Maybe the roots are edible. The flowers, though. The flowers are poisonous."

Werfel shrugged. "Maybe the flowers are poisonous. I'm not

eating the flowers. I'm eating the roots." He swished the roots back and forth in the pond to wash off some dirt, then chomped and chewed.

Spurge looked on warily. "How are they?"

"Not good. But I don't think I'll fall over backward and die."

They dug up all the gorgonbladder in the grove and washed it clean. Skardebek whizzed around the trees, delighted at all the open space where she could fly.

Werfel said, "My late fiancée — Blanchepon — she was in the army. She told me about eating gorgonbladder. When her company was fighting in the Bonecruel Mountains and their route was cut off by your Fifth Regiment."

It was clear that Spurge did not want to discuss the wars against the goblins again, or Werfel's dead girlfriend. He quietly munched his roots.

Suddenly, Skardebek squawked.

"What is it, girl?" asked Werfel, holding up his hand so she landed on it.

She had seen something while she swooped. She hopped, pointing her tentacles.

Far in the distance behind them, something glinted.

"What is that?" muttered Werfel. He affixed his spectacles to his nose. He cranked the lenses to their highest magnification and peered through them.

"Oh, dear," he said. "Oh, deary deary me."

"What is it?"

Werfel pointed. "Regibald du Burgh. He's following us somehow. And he's only a couple miles off."

Chapter 42

Throughout the long, hot afternoon they ran raggedly, side by side. They ran like scholars who were not used to running. Occasionally, Werfel would stop to suck on his robe, which still had some water soaking its folds.

"Hem?" he offered.

Spurge held up a hand for "No."

The ground was getting more hilly. There were more trees now, old and gnarled. They passed the stone ruins of goblin outposts from an age before the founding of Tenebrion.

When they were on a hilltop, Werfel turned around and

looked through his magnifying lenses. "They've stopped," he reported. "They've set up silk tents and they're sitting around eating sherbet."

"You can see the sherbet?"

Werfel admitted, "I'm just guessing about the sherbet." He frowned. "They ride vork. They know they can catch up to us whenever they want to."

"How did they find us?"

Werfel guessed, "Scent, probably. One vork knows your smell from your spying mission. And the others probably were given something from my house to sniff."

"Clothes?"

"Even worse: skins," said Werfel sadly. "All my old skins. I've lost them. I've lost my past." He turned toward the mountains and kept hiking through the dry grass. The grass hissed around his knees. He said, "The skin my dear Blanchepon once touched: gone. Probably burned up or torn apart. The cheek my mother kissed. That poor innocent boy I used to be. His skin is probably shredded to ribbons. The secret police destroyed them all, I'll wager, after getting the scent off them. Ghohg's secret police hate anyone having a history except the histories of crimes and offenses they keep in their underground files."

"It is a strange thing, this goblin shedding of skins. I must admit I am still a little disturbed by it."

"To us, it is normal. It happens every few years. It itches at first. All over your body. And you flake. But it is also a matter of pride. It means you are becoming someone new. You have grown to the point where your old shape is no longer exactly your new shape." He patted his belly. "In my case, the growth has often been here."

Spurge shook his head. "Still, it sounds uncomfortable."

"But it is a cause for celebration. Sometimes we will invite friends over and serve them hot drinks. We wish to reveal our new selves to them," he said, smiling briefly, but still sad. He was thinking about his friends back in his neighborhood, all of them gathered around the punch bowl. He thought of Druzmilla's children and the wonderful parties they had as each child split open their first skin. He concluded, "Losing my shed skins . . . It is like I have lost part of who I am."

Above them, greasy black smoke floated through the sky, smelling of burning pitch. It was unclear where it came from.

An hour later, the two scholars and the flitting icthyod paused again to look backward.

"Mr. du Burgh and his crew are back on their steeds, riding toward us," Werfel reported. "Goodness, they seem to be moving fast." He sniffed the air and said, "That's not all. Somewhere, there's a firestorm. We need to get into the mountains before it spreads."

The two ran onward, gray with dust and dirt.

"Is that the firestorm?" said Spurge, pointing.

Off to the side, there was a ruddy glow lighting the cliffs of granite. As they ran, they saw something shoulder its way upward: a spiral of flame.

One spiral gave birth to other little spirals, which coasted away, leaving burning grass in their wake.

"Oh, for an aluminum caftan!" Werfel croaked. "We need to find a place to hide."

"But if we stop moving, Mr. du Burgh and his posse will catch up to us!"

"If we don't find a good place to take shelter, we'll be burned to a crisp."

Skardebek didn't like the fire. She hovered anxiously near Werfel's ears.

"Poor little girl," said Spurge. "She's frightened."

"So am I, valued guest," muttered Werfel. "So am I."

Behind them, Regibald du Burgh's posse glinted and winked in the sunlight.

Chapter

43

Fifteen minutes later, the scholars stumbled up a steep hillside of old, ruined goblin houses. The fat stones were blackened from centuries of sun and flame.

The firestorms were getting closer, eating their way across the grass. Haze tinted the air.

Werfel said, "This must be . . . the ruins of Gargax, one of the

Six Kingdoms." He was coughing so much he had to stop and lean on an outcropping, wheezing.

At this, Skardebek wheeled away from him and soared into the sky.

Werfel shot upright. It was too dangerous for her to be flying so far with the air filled with smoke and ash. "Skardebek!" he called desperately. She was a dot high above them. He called her name again, but that started him coughing, and he couldn't speak. The air was getting sooty and hot.

Awkwardly, Spurge tried, too. "Skardebek!" he called, but not loud enough.

With a croak, Werfel got his voice again. He put his hand beside his mouth. "Come back, Bekky! Here! Here!" he demanded. "Come here right now!"

He complained, "Jerk. Never does what she's told."

He and Spurge started after her up the hill.

Gasping for breath, Werfel said, "Is that a . . . waterfall . . . up there?"

"Yes . . . I think so. . . ."

In the direction that Skardebek flew, the sheer wall of the mountain in front of them was marked by a ribbon of cool silver.

"She's . . . She's trying to get us to go that way. . . ." said Werfel.

The little icthyod now flapped back toward them. When she hit the smoke, she stumbled in the air. Werfel yelped as he saw her dive and catch herself.

Then, there she was, cruising out of the cloud, flapping toward them. Werfel held out his arms. She landed on his shoulder, coughing and terrified, nosing around his neck.

"Good awful girl," he soothed her as he ran. "Good awful girl. You found that waterfall for us."

"How far?" wheezed Spurge. "A half a mile?"

Werfel urged, "If we can only reach it . . . esteemed guest . . . then . . ." He could not finish the sentence.

Strange flakes of fire, like burning scraps of paper, drifted around them on the air. The sky was black with smoke.

Werfel's eyes stung. They would not stop watering. He wiped them with his hands, but his fingers were covered with dirt. Then his eyeballs were grimy, and he could barely see.

Spurge puffed, "Why are there so . . . many fires . . . here?"

"It is said that . . . there is a curse. . . ." Werfel considered telling the whole story, which involved feuding families, a cruel son, a jade amulet, and a burning salamander, but it didn't really seem like a good time.

With each breath, little snowflakes of floating ash choked them.

Spurge gagged. "Can't we just . . . hunker down under one of these boulders . . . and wait?"

"No . . . " explained Werfel. "Fire sucks out . . . all the . . . air. . . . If we don't find a good place to hide . . . we'll suffocate."

Spurge yelped.

An arc of flame had just shot over them like a burning cannonball and blasted into the hillside. Bushes sprang alight.

The waterfall was still almost half a mile away.

They ran along a rock wall now. They were in the shadow of the mountains, but the shadows of late afternoon hardly mattered next to the glare of flame that bloodied the stone.

The fire marched up toward them through the ancient town like something searching houses for traitors. It ate foundations and arches.

Skardebek was mewling with alarm. She had hidden herself inside Werfel's robe, pressed against his chest. He felt great pity for her. She did not understand what was happening. It was not her fault that she was going to die. It broke his heart that he could not protect her.

Fire burst out of a nearby doorway. The two scholars stumbled back.

Now a great whirlwind of flame rolled up from the plains.

The column reached up to the heavens.

The heat was overwhelming. They tried to run, but they could hardly breathe.

"Down on the ground!" Werfel shouted.

They dropped to their knees and crawled. The air near the dirt was a little clearer.

Still, Werfel knew, there was no way they would make it to the waterfall in time.

He tried to clear his mind of worry and the fear of death. Fear could not help him now.

He and Spurge flinched as flames darted all around them.

Then a stone wall collapsed.

And they were engulfed in flame.

Chapter 44

From Lord Spymaster Ysoret Clivers,
Order of the Clean Hand
To His Royal Highness, the King of Elfland

My King,

I always do so enjoy a visit to your throne room and a little chat. I'm so blessed to have you as my ruler, and while we do not seem to be on the close terms of friendship we used to be, I am delighted I can still humbly serve Your Majesty and our splendid elfin nation.

While I was in your Presence a few hours ago, we talked of strategy. You seem set on meeting with Ghohg the Evil One at the zone between our two kingdoms, at the edge of the Bonecruel Mountains. To that end, I have organized a squadron of twenty mounted griffin-riders to take you out to join General Baligant and his army. The griffin-riders will be ready to leave in two hours. Your Highness will reach the general's camp this evening. Then, tomorrow morning, you will begin the march of the final fifty miles or so to the east. Your Highness and Your Highness's army will all move forward together, but you will meet and speak with the Evil One alone. While you will have your army at the ready in case Ghohg plays dirty tricks, do not forget that Ghohg will doubtless have his goblin army ready to attack us, too. So I am just a weensy bit worried that if anything goes just the slightest smidge wrong, there will be another all-out war, worse than the last—a war like we have never seen in our lifetimes.

As you know, I was all gung-ho for war when we had a secret plan in place—when we thought that the Weed would have assassinated Ghohg by now, so that the goblins would be confused and without a ruler. But remember that now we have no special cards to play.

I know you are quite aware of that; I believe you may

even blame me and my Order for this failure, and Your Highness might even be somewhat miffed at it, given that you took the occasion of my throne room visit to have another one of my fingers removed.

While it really is good of you, old boy, to listen to my wishes, I find that I miss that pinkie more than I anticipated. Couldn't we have found a way to agree to disagree?

Wiggles Stern-Douglass was going to challenge me to a handball match later this month. Now there's no question he'll take the handball trophy for the whole country club.

Your faithful servant,

Ysoret Clivers, Lord Spymaster
Earl of Lunesse
Order of the Clean Hand

Chapter 45

Top Secret Transmission

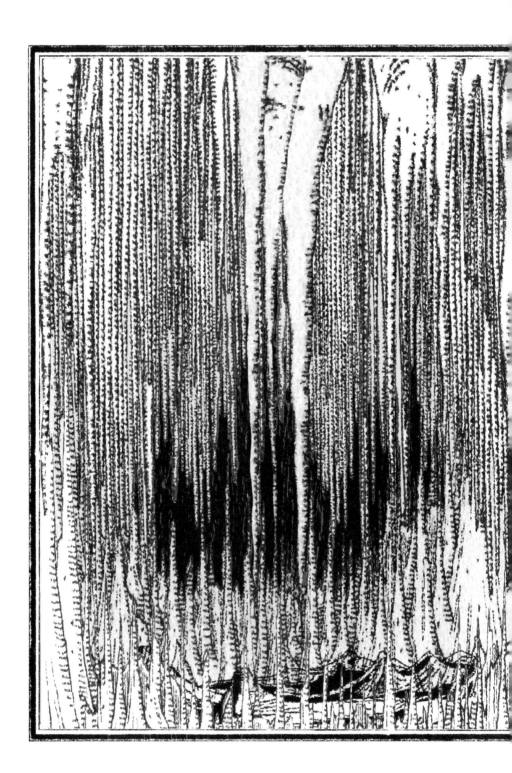

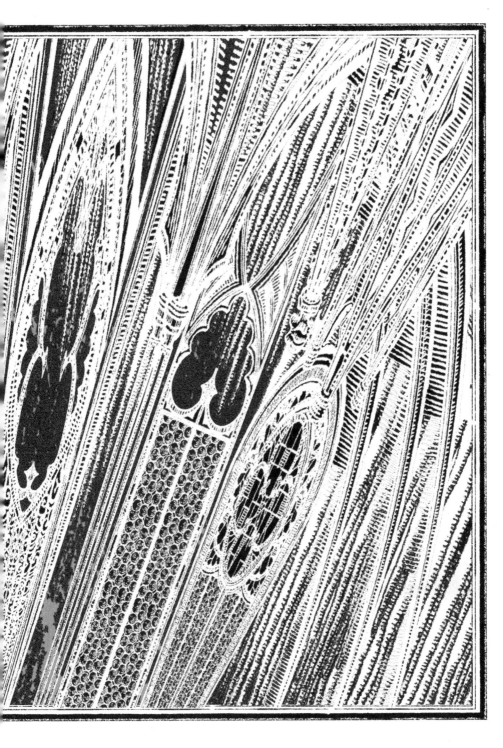

Chapter 46

Brangwain Spurge and the archivist Werfel stood for several minutes, staring around in wonder at what they could see of the underground castle that stretched above them. The towers and galleries and the dark, arched windows were filled with the rush of wind.

"Gargax," whispered Werfel. "This is one of the Six Kingdoms that rose up after the goblins fled from the forests."

"It's astounding," said Spurge. "I can't wait to tell other elfin scholars about this."

Werfel craned his neck to look up through the gloom. They walked up a grand flight of stairs. "Blanchepon and I planned to travel to the ruins of each of the Six Kingdoms on our honeymoon. That was what we were going to . . ." He stopped speaking. He shook his head to clear it.

Then, in a much more scholarly tone, he said, "This city is from before the reign of Ghohg. After the goblins fled from the elfin invasion, we founded six kingdoms, each with a fortress. At first, just little rock piles. Miserable sites where we scratched out a living and tried to hide from griffin attacks from the air. But as the centuries passed, the fortresses got more elaborate. Like this. This is very fine. Look at those remarkable arches. Imagine what this place was like filled with goblin life! But then Ghohg the Protector arrived from his world. He quickly conquered all six kingdoms. He brought us together. All the goblins finally under one banner again. Ghohg promised us strength and victory. He had us build the city of Tenebrion."

"Where are we going?" Spurge asked.

"Up. There will be passages leading us up through the heart of the mountains to the peaks. There will be observation towers looking out toward Elfland, in case of attack. During the Six Kingdoms period, there was much war. Goblin against goblin. And, as you know, goblin against elf." He squinted into the darkness. "We need to go up as quickly as we can. To lead us away from Regibald du Burgh, for one thing."

"Will he survive the firestorm?"

"Oh, yes. Why do you think he glinted? He has all the correct aluminum gear for weathering our summer flame-bursts. It will slow him down for a few hours — but when the fires burn out, he'll be able to search among the ruins and find a way into this fortress. Oh, yes, Magister Spurge, we cannot rest." Werfel pointed at an old campfire. "Look! Other visitors. Campers. Spelunkers. People do come here to holiday, though not many. It can be dangerous if the secret police discover that you've made a trip to the ruins of one of the Six Kingdoms. Ghohg is not fond of us looking back at goblin history from before he arrived."

Spurge ran his hand in wonder over some of the beautiful carvings of oak leaves and hounds and icthyods. "This is so fine. . . ." he said. "Interesting that it is much more like elfin architecture than goblin architecture. They must have based these buildings on elfin cities."

"Ah!" said Werfel. "There my distinguished guest is wrong. It is actually elfin architecture that borrowed these forms from early goblin architecture."

"How could that be?"

"Perhaps you have not read Garlunph of Drodge's *History of Towers?*"

"I believe it is referred to briefly in a far superior elfin work, Beaupierre of Lesonge's *On Castles, Keeps, and Fortresses.*"

"But I recall that Lesonge's is a much more recent book and

thus not as reliable about the early history of elfin architecture as an eyewitness account such as Tschump Weltly's *Chronicle of the Elfin Barbarians*."

"Have you ever read Melgeant Fraise's *Seven Rules of Architecture, With an Appendix on Closets*? You really should. And if you haven't, I'm not sure that you can say with authority . . ."

"Ah, or Jarud de Velsprain's *Cathedrals of Elfdom* . . . ? Very rare. Very rare, so perhaps you haven't heard of it?"

"I knew you were going to bring that up. . . . But I would recommend you read . . ."

And so, their voices echoing behind them as they climbed stairs through ancient courtyards and dormitories, they spent an almost pleasant few hours pretending to make friendly reading suggestions to each other while actually just trying to make the other feel stupid.

It was the best evening either of them had enjoyed in a very long time.

Sometimes, they paused to peer down into the chasm they'd climbed up. They did not speak at those moments, but kept silent out of a sense of wonder and lost history. Gables and towers and little turrets bristled up at them, blue and vague in their night-vision.

The wind rushing down the air shafts had died, which meant that the fires outside had probably died down, too. Neither said anything, but they were both worried that soon Regibald and his crew would be on their trail again.

They were exhausted from stairs, though. When they figured it was about midnight, they stopped to rest for a few minutes and to eat the last of their gorgonbladder roots.

They ate their scratchy meal in an old feasting hall. The walls were chiseled with fine carvings of goblin kings and queens. The two scholars sat inside a huge hooded fireplace, chewing slowly.

"Imagine the meetings that were held in this room," said Spurge, through a full mouth.

"Ah! The rulers of old," Werfel said. "Imagine the music and the dancing. The ambassadors from other realms."

"I don't know that I can eat any more of this bladder."

"Disgusting," agreed Werfel. "I've eaten too much of it today. I do not feel well. An awful weed. Oh, my stomach."

Magister Spurge looked down at the last of the gorgonbladder.

"In school," he said, "when I was a boy, they used to call me the Weed."

"That's terrible, esteemed guest."

Spurge nodded. "Because there's a weed called spurge. Common spurge."

Werfel actually felt too bad for the little-boy Spurge to even ask whether the adult Spurge had read Von Tibula's *On Flowers and the Smaller Shrubs*.

Instead, he said gently, "Remember. A weed is simply another plant."

"A plant that isn't of use. A plant no one wants."

"Those who really know plants never call things weeds. Because each plant has its special, secret uses. Every plant is a treasure to those who know them."

Spurge stared sadly into the gloom. Finally, he said, "Have you read Von Tibula's *On Flowers and the Smaller Shrubs?*"

Werfel clapped. "Ah! Esteemed guest! I was just thinking of Von Tibula!"

His clap echoed through the chamber. It sounded up and down the dead staircases that looped through the dark. Skardebek shifted nervously.

Spurge and Werfel were suddenly very aware that there was a lot of midnight around them, stacked up for miles.

Subdued, Spurge said, "We had better start to climb again."

They continued up the winding steps, past empty windows and broken balconies.

Unfortunately, Werfel's clap and shout had carried far. It had echoed through the chasm at the heart of the fortress.

So when they stepped onto a balcony and found themselves confronting a campfire and a horde of goblins with knives, there was no hiding. No backing up and just disappearing.

The glare of the flames showed scars, sneers, weapons pulled out and ready.

These were bandits. They rose from their fire and prowled forward.

Chapter 47

Ladies. Gentlemen," said Werfel. "You are doubtless simply innocent campers. We will continue upward and wish you a good night."

"You got it, pops," said a young killer, smiling. "We're just campers exploring this gloom-tastic old city."

Skardebek filled the air with angry warning yelps. Her fishy barks rang on the stone.

Backing up, Werfel said, "We would not want to trouble a gaggle of spelunking history buffs such as yourselves. As much as we would love to stay and swap stories around the campfire about old Gargax and the Six Kingdoms period, we must continue our climb."

The young killer said, "Aw, come on, pops. Let's toast some marshmallows."

Werfel stepped back again, closing his fists, ready to bean opponents if necessary. He said, "Another time, excellent campers, we will sit and have talk of the merry days of yore. I will tell you the thrilling ghost tale of Queen Glundula, whose lover fed her poison in her oatmeal. But alas, now we must go! Bekky, you terrible, squawking little scab, please be quiet. Hush. Hush. They're just campers."

The room still rang with her warning cries.

"They are actually robbers," Spurge whispered to his host unhelpfully. "Brigands. Bandits."

"Is that an elf?" roared one of the older goblins, pointing a wicked, curved sword at Spurge. Her mane of white hair was a tangle. She had death in her eyes, the haggard look of someone who has killed many times and wouldn't mind doing it again. "I hate elves," growled the woman. "Everyone hates elves. Killing an elf will be kind of fun."

"We don't want any trouble," said Werfel. "We, like you, are running from the law."

"Are you?" said the old bandit, walking over, holding the point of her curved sword near Spurge's face.

Skardebek screeched in fury.

"Someone shut that thing up," growled the bandit, "or I'll shut it up forever." She swung her scimitar toward the icthyod.

Werfel reached up and grabbed Skardebek, yanking her close to his chest. She shuddered with tiny rage.

The bandit introduced herself. "Ethelfritha the Slit-Neck," she said. "I'm expecting some fine gentlemen like you have a lot of stuff you'd like to give away free."

Werfel narrowed his eyes. "We'll give you what we have. Then you'll let us go?"

"We might. Some make it out of here. Some don't."

"Thus your name," Spurge observed. "Slit-Neck."

Ethelfritha touched her nose with the tip of her sword. "On the nose, brother," she said.

Werfel took out his wallet. "Here is everything I have with me." He opened it. "A few gold coins, some silver . . ."

The bandits surrounded both of the scholars and grabbed at them. Hands pulled and pushed.

The young man who'd first talked to them was now playing with a dagger next to Spurge. He said, "Elves are prissy. They have fine skin. Killing an elf slowly will be fun."

"Will be," Ethelfritha agreed. She ran a jagged fingernail across Spurge's cheek. "I bet he'll squeal a lot."

Spurge flinched from the dirty fingernail.

"What's the matter?" grunted Ethelfritha. "Dirty goblin touching you?"

Spurge said firmly, "And discussing my murder. I do not feel my reaction is unreasonable."

"Noble bandits!" said Werfel. "Honored goblins! I have given you all our money. We have no more to give! Please release us, as you promised."

"I didn't promise," said Ethelfritha. She grabbed Spurge by the unitard. She spit in the elf's face, then threw him backward to the floor. "No one likes an elf," said Ethelfritha. "There's no use for 'em." She kicked Spurge as hard as she could. Spurge writhed in pain.

Ethelfritha raised her scimitar to finish him off.

Chapter 48

erfel bellowed, "Stop!"

His voice was loud enough and defiant enough that everyone actually stopped. "This elf is under my protection. He is my guest. Let us go and we'll give you everything we have."

"You just said we already have everything you had."

"Here!" said Werfel, struggling out of his ceremonial robes. "Robes of the finest brocade! Worn in the highest courts of Tenebrion! Priceless!"

"Priceless?" said Ethelfritha the Slit-Neck.

Sadly folding the robes, Werfel mused, "What a strange thing is life: When I put these robes on two days ago, I thought only that we were going to be in the presence of the mighty Ghohg. Now we are fleeing for our lives . . . and these same robes will molder in the ruins of old Gargax. . . ."

He handed them over.

Werfel was left wearing only his spectacles and what looked like a giant diaper wound around his legs. His large belly hung out. He shivered with the cold of the cavern.

Ethelfritha shook the robes out and examined them. "These look expensive. Good." She sniffed them. "Aw! You've been running in these. They stink."

"Please," said Werfel, with deep emotion. "When washing, do not use hot water. They'll shrink. Stop shaking them out like that. I recommend you always take them to a cleaning professional."

"Sure," said Ethelfritha. She slung the robes over her shoulder. Then she said to her gang, "Okay. Now kill them."

"But!" Werfel protested, and Spurge squealed, "That's not fair!"

Still, the goblins surrounded them, jabbing at them with short swords and knives, forcing them back toward the balcony railing and the darkness beyond it.

Werfel looked from face to robber's face and saw only anger, hurt, hatred, and cunning. He moved backward — but there wasn't far to go. His heel found the edge of the balcony. Behind him and Spurge there was nothing but a railing and a yawning chasm.

"We won't tell anyone you're here!" Werfel said. "We would never! They'll never know!"

"No, you won't," said one of the bandits, swinging his blade near Werfel's throat. Werfel flinched backward, stumbling against a baluster.

"Get up on the railing," said Ethelfritha.

The two scholars climbed up on the stone railing, quivering at the cold draft that rose up from a half mile below. Their knees shook at the thought of the drop below them.

"Careful, now," said Ethelfritha, and she sliced her blade toward Werfel's bare legs. He danced to the side to escape, skidding on the railing, almost falling. His arms wheeled.

Another bandit appeared on his other side, swinging a scimitar. Werfel tumbled back toward Ethelfritha.

Four robbers were grouped around the elf, laughing and stabbing. Spurge shrieked and pranced desperately, trying to avoid wounds.

The two fought to keep their balance. Blades swung and

glittered in the firelight. Spurge high-stepped and jumped. Werfel almost tumbled off, but Spurge grabbed his wrist. The two were poised there, their heels over the gap.

And then Ethelfritha the Slit-Neck yelled, "Game's over! You're out!"

And goblin hands darted forward and shoved the scholars' legs.

Werfel and Spurge tottered for a minute, screamed, and then fell.

Ethelfritha held up a finger for silence.

Spurge screamed longer, his cry fading away as he disappeared into the darkness below them.

Ethelfritha nodded. "Now let's try on these robes," she said. She shrugged them on, pulling and yanking at the sleeves.

That night, as they sat around the fire eating cheddar sausages, the robbers were in awe of Ethelfritha. They had always known she was a born leader; but now, smiling and triumphant in fine court garments, she looked like a queen.

Chapter

49

Werfel and Spurge were lucky there was another balcony right below them, so they only fell ten feet. Spurge was even luckier: he landed on Werfel. His cry faded as he realized he wasn't going to die.

Werfel, on the other hand, was stunned by the fall. His breath was knocked out of him. He lay with his arms spread wide, gulping at the air, unable to speak or breathe.

The stone was so cold on his bare back it felt like it burned.

Spurge thought quickly, putting his finger over his lips and trying to help Werfel to his feet quietly. Their lives depended on their silence. They could hear the bandits cackling on the floor above.

Bent over in pain, Werfel staggered away from the balcony. Spurge supported him. Skardebek clung to his shoulder, licking his cheek with worry. They crept through a ruined chapel, then into dark corridors.

For twenty minutes, they walked without speaking.

When they were far away from the bandits, they traded a few careful whispers.

Spurge said, "Archivist, I apologize deeply for landing on top of you."

"It was not your intention."

"You must be freezing, Archivist, without clothes."

Suddenly, much to Spurge's surprise, he saw Werfel grin.

"I am," said Werfel. "And it is a good thing, too. That is the only good thing that came out of that terrifying encounter."

Spurge's forehead creased. "I don't understand."

"Honored guest," Werfel explained with glee, "we are being tracked by vork who know our smell. And I just gave a robe — soaked with my own personal sweat — to a group of evil bandits." He rubbed his hands together. "We have just thrown Regibald du Burgh, as the saying goes, completely off the scent. When he seeks us, he shall find Ethelfritha the Slit-Neck."

Chapter 50

At around dawn, the two scholars stumbled out of a broken tower on top of the Bonecruel Mountains.

Werfel could not stop shivering. He emerged from the caverns almost naked, swaddled in his linen diaper like a warty baby. He had never felt so cold in his life. His skin burned. His teeth clacked together. His beard was all that warmed him, and he clutched it to his chest. Little Skardebek wouldn't settle on his shoulder because his shivering bothered her.

They saw the sun rising over the country of the goblins. It lit the lofty places in the mountains, the ravines filled with pines, the pointy crags of granite.

"You are a strange color of blue," said Spurge.

Through a quivering jaw, Werfel said, "Let's keep going."

"Don't worry," said Spurge. "Soon the sun will warm you."

They followed a path into the deep pine forest. Spurge said, "The design of old Gargax really is remarkably similar to the later elfin castle of Fonceney, far to the south of here. I cannot wait to get back to Dwelholm and write a paper about this. Early cultural exchange between elves and goblins. You have opened my eyes. I have so many questions to ask. And to think, I am the first elf to have seen the ruins of Gargax for centuries!"

Werfel wasn't even listening. He couldn't keep walking. His body was too cold. It was shutting down. He sagged against a pine and sat.

"I am sorry, esteemed guest," he said. "I cannot go on."

Spurge was alarmed. "We'll make you a fire!" he said. He started to crack the black lower limbs off pines.

"It might give away our position to others," Werfel protested.

"You need to warm up." Spurge kept filling his arms with sticks.

"All right. Maybe just a quick fire. Just . . ."

"Sit down, Archivist."

Werfel muttered, "Oh, oh . . . how will we light a campfire?"

Spurge had made a little pile of leaves, then twigs, then sticks, then logs.

"Oh, little Bekky," said Werfel. "Your friend and master is so cold. How will we light the fire?"

Spurge frowned and looked around the clearing. Then he said, "We'll use your lenses. Archivist, please?"

Shivering, Werfel removed his spectacles and handed them over. Spurge cranked them to maximum magnification. He tilted the spectacles back and forth to catch the early sunshine. At first, nothing happened.

But shortly, the leaves under the magnifier started to smolder.

A few minutes later, they had a fire going. The goblin in his underwear scooched dangerously close to it and held his arms around it.

"Do watch out for your beard," said Spurge. "You'll go up in flames."

The elf rushed off to gather more wood. Werfel huddled by the flame, shivering. He hoped that they were safe for a while. Surely the combination of fire, smoke, the stink of caverns, and bandits with decoy sweat would conceal their scent. It would take Regibald du Burgh a long, long time to find them now.

There was a crash of bushes, a tumbling figure.

It was Spurge. As he burst into the clearing, he let out a huge gasp. "I stole!" he exclaimed. "There was a cabin on stilts with laundry hung out to dry. I gathered my courage and I stole some sheets for you to wear, Archivist! Here, sir!"

He held out a mess of tangled sheets.

"I cannot thank you enough, esteemed guest," said the Archivist, stiffly rising from his little fire. "Though the sheets have little dollies on them."

They dressed him in the embroidered linens. Werfel wrapped one sheet around him like a cloak. He used a pillow-case as a cap. He fought with the second sheet for a while, but eventually it became a kind of jacket. He hid his freezing hands inside it.

"This will allow me to continue our march to your pickup point," said Werfel.

"Yes. You will be fine," said Spurge. "Perhaps we can even ask the griffin-riders to take you back with me." He suddenly hit on an idea. "We can write the book about early elf-goblin cultural exchange together! It will be a work such as never has been written before!"

"We should keep walking, now that I am warmer," said Werfel. They started slowly down the path. Werfel moved heavily.

"I have seen things no elf has seen and lived to tell about," said Spurge. "I may have failed on my diplomatic mission, but I have so much to tell my people!"

Out of kindness or cold, Werfel said nothing in reply. He did not repeat his doubts about whether the royal government of Elfland would really send help. He thought, however, about how lonely people in mountains yodel to the empty peaks and take the echo for a friendly reply.

They kept on walking along the ridge of the mountains. They went through chilly forests of spruce and fir, and scrambled over rock faces. Werfel calculated that they needed to keep going north.

They had to be very careful about running into goblins. There were lonely cabins and stone cottages in the heights, and guard towers manned by Ghohg's soldiers. They even saw a little goblin village in one valley, with lumberjacks hauling huge trees through on wagons.

It all looked so peaceful — but to stop at any of these places would mean almost certain death for an elf like Brangwain Spurge.

Another time, they passed by the ruins of a town that had been destroyed during the recent war with the elves. Wildflowers grew in the fallen houses; where the corpses of goblin families had fallen, there were mushroom clumps.

Later in the afternoon, they rested at a spot where they

could look out to the east over the Plateau of Drume. Werfel arranged his sheets to cushion him on the granite.

"From here, we'll head west," he explained. "By this evening, we should be looking down the other side of the mountains toward Elfland. That's where the glass tower is."

"What is that?" asked Spurge, pointing. "Out in the plains . . . Is that smoke? Another firestorm down there?"

Werfel squinted through the magnifying spectacles. "No . . . " he said. "No, look." Urgently, he handed Spurge the lenses.

Spurge did look, and he saw that there, in the midst of the plain, a goblin army was on the march. Dust rose from the horde.

There were thousands of them, all in neat ranks. Companies of knights rode armored horses or vork. Infantrymen carried pikes and halberds. Above them in the sky, war-wyverns screamed.

And far back, under a huge tent of silk and brocade and cloth of gold, shining with a weird, otherworldly light, was Ghohg, being rolled across the desert on a gilded platform.

"Oh, no," said Werfel. "What do you think is happening?"

"History, Archivist," said the elf miserably. "What is happening is history."

Chapter 51

From Lord Spymaster Ysoret Clivers,
Order of the Clean Hand
To His Royal Highness, the King of Elfland

Your Highness,

I understand that you have reached General Baligant's army and you are on the march east toward the Bonecruel Mountains. I shall be joining you soon.

Our wizard has just received a message from the court of Ghohg. The goblins are expecting a ceremonial exchange of gifts before the parley. Of course, we had a gift prepared for the Evil One—and what a gift!—the cursed gemstone—but it has been lost. Yes, Your Highness, I understand that you are peeved about that. The missing bits of my right hand often remind me of your displeasure.

But still, we must find some piece of glittery trash to give the king of the goblins. Something that will please him but won't be much of a loss. We need someone to have a bit of a wander through the royal treasury, looking at all the ancient artifacts, and tell us which one has a bit of razzle-dazzle to it but won't make us cry when we miss it down the road. I wish we had the old Weed here. He'd know.

Yes, Your Majesty, I realize that I am the one who sent the incompetent Weed off into the wild. Once again, recall, I have gaps in my hand to remind me.

By the by, the poor Weed still sends updates. This time, visions of a firestorm—really, the land of the goblins is clearly an endlessly wretched place, and they must be awful creatures to want to live there. To wish to make a life in that wasteland of rock and flame, you'd have to be a beast without a sense of beauty, hope, or joy. No one with a soul could live in such a place.

These are the terrible creatures you ride forth to meet, Your Majesty.

In the next few days, I shall fly out to be by your side for your confrontation with Ghohg the Evil One. I shall not be secure holding the reins of my griffin, but I shall still grip your hand in greeting, Your Highness, to convince you I am always

Your humble servant,

Ysoret Clivers, Lord Spymaster
Earl of Lunesse
Order of the Clean Hand

Chapter 52

The elfin spy and his goblin host hiked through the Bonecruel Mountains toward the old glass tower. The path led through meadows and forests.

They were both very hungry. They'd run out of roots to eat. Werfel was not used to exercise, and he huffed and puffed a lot, lumbering over rocks and roots.

Late in the afternoon, they crested a dome of stone and found themselves staring out at Elfland. Down the mountain slopes it lay, spread before them with its green fields, its orchards, its forests, its rivers and lakes, where white sails drifted.

At the top of the mountain was a white pole marking the border between Elfland and the domain of the goblins, defiantly flying the flag of Ghohg.

"Ah, beautiful Elfland!" Spurge exclaimed. "My home! I am almost home, Archivist!"

Werfel tried to smile enthusiastically, but he was thinking that he himself could never go home. And if he did go back, he would not be going to any neighborhood parties or skin-shedding jamborees. He would be arrested and executed. Druzmilla would have to pretend to hate him, or she and her children would be suspected of helping an enemy of Ghohg escape. The rest of the neighborhood — bakers, fletchers, candle-makers, booksellers, builders, painters, other historians — would have to pretend they had never been friends with him in the first place.

Spurge gushed, "There is a gorgeous glow to my country this evening."

The wind whapped at the flag. "It will be growing cold soon," said Werfel grimly. "Night is almost fallen."

"I'm sorry, Archivist," said Spurge, though he was not responsible for night.

"Ah, well," said Werfel, lowering the flag. "We can at least warm ourselves with this." He untied it from its rope. He slung it around Spurge's shoulders. "This is the greatest hospitality my nation can give you right now, esteemed guest."

That night, after the sun had gone down, they used the canvas flag as a blanket. Neither one relished the smell of the other. And it was too small for both of them, so they fought over who should get more fabric. Both of them insisted the other should use it.

"You take a little more of the flag, treasured guest."

"No, Archivist. You will be colder than I will. You take a little more."

"I insist, Magister." They shoved the flag back and forth.

Skardebek slept between them, snoring louder than either. She, at least, was warm and safe.

Each of the scholars, without telling the other, woke up at some point during the night and made sure the other one was covered, then watched for a while to make sure the three of them were safe from anything that might slink through the woods in darkness.

In this way, wrapped in the colors of the nation that sought their death, they slept until well past dawn.

Later that morning they came to the glass tower.

Chapter 53

At around ten they spotted it twinkling on a nearby ridge. It took a while to get to it: first they had to scramble down into a deep river valley and then up again through the pines.

Spurge was miserably scratching himself. He had accidentally slept in a patch of poison ivy and was itchy and grumpy.

It was almost noon when they reached the shattered tower itself. Giant shards stuck up from the mountaintop. There were still spiral staircases of glass leading to thin bridges in the air. Everywhere lay sharp, broken remains, glittering in the noonday sun.

Beyond the tower, Elfland lay below them, golden with haze.

"Elfland . . ." said Spurge with a sigh. "My homeland. I'll be back down there soon. In the great white marble halls of the library at Dwelholm. Oh, Archivist, you cannot imagine the beauty of that place!"

Werfel just grimaced.

"We will exchange books," said Spurge. "There will be wonderful traffic in knowledge between our two nations now. We will understand each other's histories."

They walked around the gleaming shell of broken glass.

Spurge quizzed his host. "You said Ghohg ordered your people to build these towers?"

"Yes. Most of them in the desert. Then, ten or fifteen years later, he told work teams to knock them down, one by one. No one knows why. We probably wouldn't understand the reason if he told us."

"So much work . . . It must have been beautiful."

"Watch out. Your feet will get cut."

They settled themselves in some soft moss at the edge of the forest, once they'd checked it for pellets of glass.

Werfel kept watch while Spurge, crackling with magical fire and hovering above the ground, sent a signal back to Dwelholm telling them he had arrived at the meeting spot.

"It probably takes six or seven hours to get here by griffin," the elf said. "They should be here this evening to pick me up."

Werfel nodded, but he just seemed sad and quiet.

Brangwain Spurge was almost vibrating with excitement. He clearly couldn't wait to be picked up and to go home. Everything in his trip to the kingdom of the goblins seemed more like a charming adventure now that he was about to leave. He even admitted he'd liked a few of the dishes they tried at Tenebrion's restaurants.

He asked Werfel to tell him more about Old Goblinish — a language he didn't know — and Werfel admitted he couldn't really make out Old Elven. They talked about food words in those thousand-year-old languages and licked their lips over the ancients' words for "oranges" and "deep-fried." They swapped stories of their nations' great books and made plans to trade old manuscripts one day, so they could better understand the history of their two races a thousand years before. They chattered companionably about the distant past, waiting for the golden griffins to appear in the sky.

They almost didn't hear the steps approaching them through the brush.

They fell silent, worried it might be goblins from a guard outpost.

Spurge hissed, "Maybe it's Lord Clivers!"

Werfel looked grim. "They're not coming," he whispered. "It's more likely goblins than elves."

"I don't know why you must be so grim and pessimistic."

"Because I know how noblemen, politicians, and rich people work."

"You have no faith in me! You do not realize my value to the elfin kingdom!"

"I have no —"

But then a high, light voice called out Spurge's name. "Magister Brangwain Spurge?" And then, in Elven, "Magister, where are you? We've come a long way looking for you!"

Spurge stood. "Here I am!" he said, jumping up from the moss. "I am honored you sought me out!"

Then he fell silent. Because what greeted him was not a cluster of elfin knights dressed in griffin-riding gear.

"I am in the happy-sauce we finded you!" said the high voice in bad Elven.

Because it was not an elf at all, but Regibald du Burgh.

Chapter

54

In his normal voice, which was quite deep, and in his usual language, which was Goblinish, Regibald du Burgh growled, "You lost us for a while, elf. Good work. But the bounty on your head is high and the vork don't sleep." The vork screamed and strained at their leashes. "You can't take off the smell of your own elf sweat as easily as clothes."

There were fifteen goblins there — jeering athletes who were clearly used to fighting. Eight were required just to hold back the crazed vork. The rest were preparing for carnage.

Regibald du Burgh grabbed a giant mace, knobbed with spikes, from a squire.

"You're going to kill him now, aren't you?" said one of Regibald's henchmen.

"I have a debt of honor to settle," Regibald explained to Spurge. "And as it happens, when I take your head back to Ghohg, I'll get a nice little pile of gold, too."

Spurge stumbled backward. "You know," he said, "you'll get much more money if you bring me back alive. I have so many . . . so many secrets I could tell Ghohg. About the kingdom of the elves. And the Order of the Clean Hand. Do you know of the Order? Top secret, of course, but I know it all."

"You're disgusting," said Regibald. "Willing to sell out your own country just to save your life."

This irritated Spurge. "As it happens," he snapped, "I was going to lie to you anyway."

Du Burgh raised his mace. "No time left for that now," he said.

He prepared to smash the elf into pulp.

At this, there was a rattle in the bushes, and Werfel

appeared — "Hold, you scoundrel du Burgh!" — hopping on one leg, trying to untangle his bedsheets from the bushes. With dignity, he stepped between Regibald du Burgh and his prey.

"Regibald du Burgh! I, Archivist Werfel, formerly in the service of His Fearsome Majesty Ghohg the Protector, am the host and guardian of Brangwain Spurge. He is a guest in my home."

"Your house has been burned to the ground and they are building a public restroom on the ashes," Regibald informed him. "You are a man with no home and no skins."

Werfel blanched at this news. But still, he steeled himself and said, "I do not believe you. But still, it would not matter! A home is not simply a place! It is also an offer of hospitality, an agreement to protect my guests, whomever they may be!" He clomped forward, dragging a large rhododendron branch that was caught in his sheet. "When I agreed to take the elfin envoy and scholar Brangwain Spurge into my house, I swore to shield him with my life. You shall not take him, sir; you shall not lay a finger on a hair of his head or his pointed ears, sir — you shall not even raise your weapon against him — without killing me first."

Regibald shrugged. "Okay," he said.

Werfel sighed. He didn't like what was coming next.

"Regibald du Burgh," he said, "I challenge you to a duel, you cowardly, lily-livered, stitch-faced desperado. Your boasts are empty and your facial hair is pathetic. So much for the ritual insults. Now, stand still while I kick you between the legs."

Werfel could not see Spurge — who was behind him. He could only see du Burgh, who grinned wolfishly. Standing there, wearing his stupid doll-print sheets, about to die for the pesky elf he'd risked so much to save, fighting a nobleman who, under other circumstances, might have been a great ally, Werfel wished his life were not going to end this way. He knew he had to do the right thing, but he was not happy about it.

Sweat crossed his brow. He'd wanted to grow older, to write a book on goblin-elf relations throughout history. He'd wanted to play games with Skardebek on the rooftop and call out loud, obnoxious "Halloo"s down to the neighbors. He'd wanted to read books by candlelight while the snow fell outside and Skardebek snored on his knee. Maybe he even wanted, someday, to fall in love again. It seemed unfair that his one chance at being alive should end so stupidly.

Regibald du Burgh announced, "I accept the challenge of the once-archivist Werfel, traitor to his own people, elf-friend, patsy for the enemy."

The whole assembled group followed as Werfel carefully

picked his way among the giant curls and shards of broken glass with Regibald, dressed in full armor, clanking behind him.

Skardebek tried to follow Werfel, mewling.

"No, girl," said Werfel, scratching her bobbing head. "You stay back." He leaned forward and kissed her.

The other goblins burst out laughing and making kissy noises.

Werfel didn't care. "You've always been a good girl," he said to his faithful icthyod. "A good, awful girl." He looked deep into her black, loving eyes.

With that, he left her and confronted the noble bully and his horde.

The two goblins stood near the base of the broken glass tower. The sun caught on the sharp edges and shone like the air was gold. To the one side towered the Bonecruel Mountains. To the other lay the warm lowlands of Elfland.

"What is your weapon?" Regibald said.

"Let it be understood," said Werfel. "If I defeat you, none of your friends or followers has the right to come after me or my guest. Your blood will clear all debts of honor."

He was not comfortable with all the laughter that followed his declaration. Clearly, Regibald's friends expected Werfel to die pretty quickly.

"Sure," Regibald answered. "You don't have a weapon, do you?"

Glumly, Werfel said, "No, Your Lordship."

"But I do," said a defiant voice with an elfish accent.

And there stood Magister Brangwain Spurge, his face set in calm anger. In his hands, he held a snapped glass pillar with a wicked point.

"This fine goblin," said Spurge, pointing at Werfel, "has taken every abuse for me. He has lost his house, his friends, his livelihood, and his life for me. And he did not even like me. He did it only because he is kind in the face of insult and honorable even when betrayed. He is one of the best people I have ever met. I cannot let Archivist Werfel die for my mistakes. Regibald du Burgh, you may be twice as tall as him, but you are half the person he is. And so, sir — you bully — you coward — I challenge you to a fight to the death, right here and now."

Regibald rolled his eyes. "One of you, the other of you, I don't care. Whichever one wants to die, step forward."

Eyeing each other furiously, both scholars stepped forward.

"Let me," said Spurge. "You have done nothing but protect me from my own mistakes."

And with that, he raised the glass pillar like a spear and charged.

Chapter 55

Top Secret Transmission

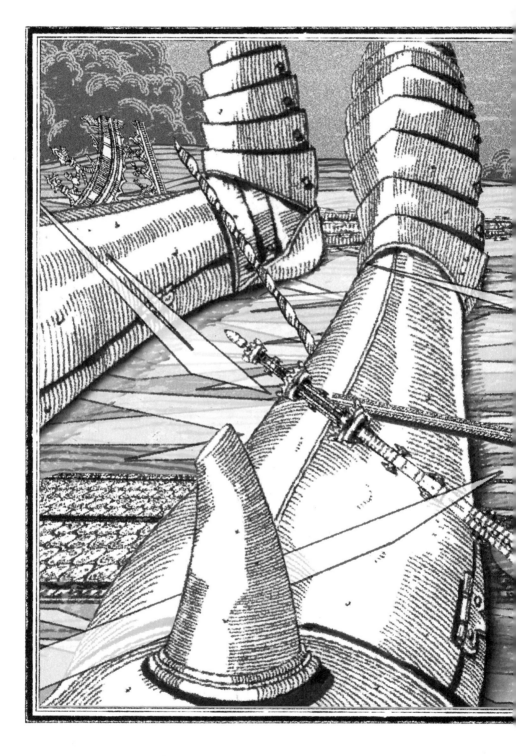

Chapter 56

Archivist Werfel and Magister Brangwain Spurge perched on rocks high above the glass tower, hidden by cedars, and waited for something to happen.

A few hours earlier, they had watched as a few of Regibald du Burgh's gang had picked up their boss on a stretcher and carried him off. He was dangerously near death from his fall.

"If they come back again to find us," said Spurge, "we will be gone. Flying through the air."

Werfel wrapped his arms around his legs and leaned against the rough bark of the cedars.

"Will you come with me?" said Spurge.

In a subdued voice, Werfel said, "If you go, Magister Spurge, I will miss you, but I am not sure my future lies in Elfland."

"You still think my own government will abandon me," said Spurge with a little bitterness. "You believe my own Elf King will not save one of his most loyal servants. Someone who has risked life and limb for him, and seen inside the city of the goblins."

Werfel did not want to hurt his guest's feelings, so he simply said, "I will miss you, Brangwain Spurge."

Spurge almost smiled. He said, "And I will miss you, Archivist Werfel."

They watched the sun set behind the hills of Elfland. It turned that rich kingdom gold and brass. Spurge gathered the flag close around him to keep himself warm.

"I will get to see my dear aged parents again," he said. "My father was a poor clerk, and my mother, Euphorbia, was a seamstress in the royal palace. She sewed dresses for the palace maids. Once she sewed the table runner for the feasting table of the Elf King himself."

"I am sure your family misses you very much."

"And now I shall go back and show my fellow elves that the child of a clerk and a seamstress is as good and brave as the most famous knight in the kingdom." He nodded. "I'll show everybody. All the high and mighty. The boys who tormented me at school."

"They called you The Weed."

Spurge looked embarrassed. "I should not have told you. But yes, that is what they called me. Lord Ysoret Clivers, who now is His Majesty's spymaster — he used to be one of the worst. I feared him and hated him in silence. Now I will show him that I am his equal. I am as much an elf as he."

Werfel said quietly, "Don't count on him noticing."

"You have not seen the beauty, intelligence, and gentility of the elfin nobility."

"Snow glitters most when it is coldest."

"The riders will be here for me at any minute," said Spurge. "We cannot see them because the light is failing."

And the stars came out above the two, and swung in the heavens.

No one came for Brangwain Spurge.

Chapter 57

From Lord Spymaster Ysoret Clivers,
Order of the Clean Hand
To His Royal Highness, the King of Elfland

Your Highness,

By the time you get this letter, I will be on griffin-back, flying
out to meet you and the army.

We have, at long last, selected a gift for Ghohg. We have
chosen an old sword, just rusty enough to look important.

Some lovely little engraved knots and vines on it. I'm sure we can pass it off as magical.

Here is what we have agreed with the goblins: When you meet with Ghohg, both you and he will be permitted only two attendants, to ensure that there are no tricks. Both armies will have to stay well back for the parley. I suggest that you take your Royal Champion and myself.

Speaking of your Royal Champion, I wonder if you might have a word with him. While I realize that Your Majesty continues to be angry at me for flubbing the plan, I don't really think it's playing fair badminton to have your champion remove more than one finger for each error. When he appeared this morning, therefore, and demanded I spread out my hand, I really let him know I was not pleased with the situation, and owed him not a single finger more.

Thus, I enclose my thumb.

In other news, the Weed continues to send useless updates of his trials in the kingdom of the goblins. Most recently, he sent me an utter fantasy in which he faces off against a goblin knight and somehow wins. I think the little twerp is just trying to get my sympathy. He always was a miserable little crybaby, and clearly nothing has changed. He obviously thinks we're coming to fetch him. Being stranded in the land of death is a little rotten for him, but there's nothing we can do. What can he be thinking? If I could respond to him, I'd say, Stop sniveling and die somehow already. I want him off my conscience.

I will keep this letter brief, as it is difficult to write in my present circumstances.

Your humble servant,

Ysoret Clivers, Lord Spymaster
Earl of Lunesse
Order of the Clean Hand

The moon came out above the two scholars. It softly lit both the little villages of Elfland and the mountain outposts of the goblins, as if the whole world were at peace.

"Archivist Werfel?" said the elf.

"Yes, Magister Spurge?"

"I am truly sorry. I am truly, truly sorry for all I have done to you."

"I know you are, esteemed guest."

The moon picked out crystals in the broken tower of glass.

Spurge said, "You never accepted my apology."

Werfel smiled. "Magister Brangwain Spurge, I accept your apology." He held out his warty hand.

Spurge held out his.

And there on the mountaintop between the two kingdoms, beneath their one moon, elf and goblin shook hands.

Then they waited some more.

Spurge explained, "I just wanted to say that, before I left."

Werfel did not reply.

Spurge scratched his poison ivy.

Sometime, the moon went down.

Nobody came.

Chapter

59

Werfel awoke. He couldn't guess what time it was because Skardebek had fallen asleep plastered to his face, her tentacles clamped over his eyes, nose, and mouth. He peeled her off, despite her protests, and spat and rubbed at his mouth as hard as he could.

"Bekky! Bekky! You terrible vermin," he said. "Disgusting!"

He was just about to call out a friendly "Good morning!" when he noticed that a little ways off through the trees, Spurge was sitting on the pine needles and crying.

"What's wrong?" he said, going to the scholar's side.

Spurge shook his head.

Werfel said, "They didn't come overnight."

Spurge shook his head again.

"Magister Spurge, I am sorry."

"You warned me."

"I wish it were different."

"They still think I'm just a weed. To be thrown away when you've picked it. When you've yanked it up from the bed where it grew."

"You cannot trust the wealthy and powerful."

"I thought I would be useful," wept Spurge. "I thought I could be different than I was. I thought I could be one of them."

"You were useful," said Werfel. "But just because you're useful to the wealthy doesn't mean they'll reward you. It just means they'll use you."

Spurge's nose was running. "What have I done?" he said. "I betrayed the one person who was kind to me to help people who threatened me. And I wasn't even good at betraying. I messed up everything for everyone. I'm alone now, and sore from running, and bleeding from walking on glass, and I have poison ivy . . . and I'm hungry. So hungry."

His face crinkled and he sobbed.

"I will go down to one of the villages we passed yesterday," Werfel offered. "I'll bring back some food for both of us."

"It is too kind of you, Archivist Werfel."

"It is not kind," Werfel explained. "Crying people make me nervous."

Thumping a walking stick on the ground, he retraced their route of the day before back into the forest. Skardebek followed. They came to a settlement of a few goblin houses and a squat guard tower overlooking the kingdom of the elves. There, Werfel presented himself at the door of the tower.

"Oh, alas, alas!" He begged, "Do you have work for a poor wandering goblin who has lost everything?"

He spent the morning stacking firewood in exchange for two slices of venison-pickle jelly. His stomach was queasy with hunger. Meanwhile, Skardebek played with the guards, skating over their heads while they threw her pellets of bread.

Toward lunchtime, Werfel finished his work, and the quartermaster gave him two sticky slices of venison-pickle jelly, one splopped in each hand. It was not easy to walk with both of them, so he ate one, licking his palm clean with hunger when he was done.

He hiked back to the glass tower to deliver the other slice to sad Spurge.

But when he got back to the ledge where they had hidden out, Spurge was gone.

He looked around. Skardebek dodged between the trees, chirping.

"Surely they could not have come . . . ?" Werfel muttered. Then he worried that something had happened to Spurge. Maybe du Burgh's friends had returned.

Frantic, Werfel ran from one end of the clearing to the other, calling Spurge's name.

Beneath it all, he was worried that perhaps the elfin knights had come to collect his friend — and that Spurge hadn't even bothered to say good-bye.

He ran past the glass ruins and called, "Magister Spurge!" out to the mountains and valleys. His own voice echoed back.

Werfel paused to catch his breath, almost in tears. The venison-pickle jelly melted in his hand.

Then he thought he heard Spurge's voice in the distance, calling his name.

Werfel went to the ledge. He looked out over Elfland.

He was astonished. A mighty army was on the move.

This time, it was an elfin army. Their banners of silk billowed in the breeze. Their musicians blew horns, and even from this height, he could hear their elegant melodies. Griffins flew back and forth in the sky, cawing, while knights sitting on their backs brandished lances, spears, and bows.

And there, bounding down the side of the mountain, his scrawny arms flapping, the flag tied around his neck like a cape, was Brangwain Spurge.

Spurge stopped for a moment, looked back up toward Werfel, and called out faintly, "Archivist! It is the elfin army! They're here!" Then he continued hopping from stone to stone down the mountainside.

"Avoid them!" Werfel yelled back. Then, to Skardebek, he said, "Oh, dear."

He started down the path after Brangwain Spurge, lumbering from stone to stone.

The three of them leaped through dark forests of fir and spruce.

It was hard for Werfel to carry a handful of venison-pickle jelly while bounding along, so he thought it was best to eat it. It was delicious.

He held up his hand as he ran so Skardebek could drop down and lick the remains of the slime off.

Lower down the mountain, they ran through forests of oak and maple. Spurge plunged through first. About ten minutes later, Werfel followed, huffing and puffing and dragging his sheets. Skardebek squeaked above his head.

He was too late, however.

By the time Werfel got to the bottom of the mountain,

Spurge had joyously greeted his nation's army. He had called out his bright "Greetings and salutations, fellow elves!" He had completely forgotten that he was wearing the flag of the enemy, the sign of Ghohg, strapped around his neck.

And Werfel? Werfel was a goblin.

Knights with wings on their helmets sprang out around the two. They held them at spear point.

Skardebek, shrieking, flew at the knights.

"No, Bekky!" Werfel screamed — but it was too late.

One of the guards swung a sword and hit her with the flat. Werfel heard the crunch. Skardebek went whirling over their heads and hit the ground. She lay there twitching as the knights pulled their two prisoners away.

"Bekky! Bekky!" Werfel was almost choked with rage and anguish.

He could no longer see her, though, because he was surrounded by a thicket of weapons.

Stunned, he and Spurge were dragged toward the camp of the Elf King.

Chapter

Τhe elfin camp crawled with activity. Soldiers marched up and down the rows of white canvas tents. The horses were scared of the griffins. Page boys ran to and fro between the colorful silk pavilions of the nobles, carrying messages.

In one of the gray tents of the Order of the Clean Hand, Spurge and Werfel sat slumped in a metal cage, waiting to hear news of their doom.

Werfel could not stop worrying about Skardebek, little Skardebek, Bekky. His Bekks. The poor, awful little girl. He twisted his beard in his hands.

Then a cheerful voice said, "Hello, Weeds, old stick," and Spurge jumped. A noble elf strode into the gray tent, wearing robes of costly damask. Around his neck was a medallion: the symbol of the Clean Hand. Oddly enough, Werfel noticed, the man's own right hand was wrapped up in bloodied gauze.

The man said, "Yes, Weedy, it's me." The nobleman introduced himself to Werfel: "Lord Ysoret Clivers, head of His Majesty's intelligence service." He extended his left hand through the bars toward Werfel. Werfel stared at it in confusion. "To shake, you silly thing. Not to bite off." He shook his head in disgust. "Goblins . . ."

Two guards brought forward a chair for Clivers to sit on. The spymaster sat back and crossed his legs, looking at his two prisoners with faint amusement.

"You both look a little glum, chums. But buck up: no need to worry about what's going to happen to you."

"Really?" said Spurge.

"Of course not, Weeds. It's death. Sentence: execution by beheadment." He smiled. "Load off your mind, I'm sure. Lucien, could I have one of those chocolates? I prefer the caramel centers."

As he chewed, he said, "Now, we don't have much time, because we want to execute you quickly. Complex reasons. I don't wish to bore you at a time like this. You don't have long left for listening, anyway. I expect you'll want to make the most of each precious moment by thinking of your mumsy or the beauty of a summer's day in June.

"So what I'd like to do is ask you some questions. Normally, this is where we'd include the torture, but we simply haven't enough hours in the day. Weeds, you were sent as a spy. Now is your chance to show us what you learned. If it is useful, I may spare your life. At dawn, our beloved Elf King — may he reign forever and so forth — will meet upon a nearby field with Ghohg the Evil One. Depending on how that talk goes, our two armies may well rush at each other for days of savage bloodletting. What we'd prefer to do is win.

"Any hints, Weedy? Anything we should know?"

"Will you . . . will you spare the goblin, too?"

"No, we won't spare the goblin. Death. Beheadment. But we will note that you've become a goblin-friend, putting the life of a goblin above the needs of your own kingdom."

Spurge's head dropped. "What do you want to know?" he asked quietly.

"So many things. How many soldiers there are in Ghohg's army. How the Well of Lightning works. What is the best way to capture the city of Tenebrion. Why you're wearing the flag of the enemy around your neck. Even just who this wretched goblin is."

He snapped (with his good hand), and a spy in a black hood

brought out a large stack of illustrations. Ysoret Clivers flipped through them, pulling out a few to show the two prisoners. "These are the illustrations you sent back to our device. Look at them."

Spurge did look at them. And he was ashamed.

Werfel looked at them, too, bewildered. These were the images Spurge had sent back to his homeland? They were unrecognizable. All of his wonderful neighbors — they looked wicked as monsters. They were leering and hungry. The adorable little cadet scouts looked like savage miniature killers. For some reason, the women in the flower parade had their heads lopped off. And someone was flinging people's skulls out an upstairs window — more likely a turkey carcass or a ham bone. The buildings didn't even always look like goblin buildings. None of it looked like what it really was. And . . . was that supposed to be him?

"You sent images of your goblin guide," said Ysoret Clivers, "but this is clearly not him. You showed him taller than you. This little toad is shorter and doesn't look like he could hurt a fly. But they share a beard. So . . . if this isn't your guide, who is he? And if he is your guide, what other errors have you made in your transmissions?"

Werfel looked over at Spurge. He couldn't believe that Spurge had recently imagined him that way, hideous and growling. Werfel had been doing nothing but trying to make Spurge's stay as pleasant and informative as possible, opening up his home, his city, and his heart to this emissary, and yet here he was, drawn as a caricature, a goofy, cruel-looking buffoon. And everything he loved, everything he had shown the visiting elf was turned into a grotesque cartoon, a bloody comedy of violence.

This was the elf he was about to die for.

Somehow, he had known this was what Spurge thought of him. It just hurt to have it there in front of him, drawn starkly in black ink.

"Weeds?" snapped the lounging spymaster. "What'll it be? Life or death?"

And so Magister Brangwain Spurge, unsuccessful assassin, leaned forward with his elbows on his scrawny knees and began to make his full confession.

Chapter 01

No," said Spurge. "Of course this isn't that terrible guide. This is Werfel. He's the leader of the Goblin Resistance."

"What resistance?"

"It's an underground movement . . . to fight Ghohg the Evil One from the inside. . . . That's why I brought him to you. . . . So you could . . . work with him . . ."

"This is true?" Clivers asked Werfel. "You are the head of the Goblin Resistance?"

Werfel nodded. Then he thought he should do something

heroic and resistant, so he raised his fist in defiance and said, "Death to tyrants."

"Ah," said Clivers. "This fellow looks a little short and stout to be the leader of the Goblin Resistance."

"But he's fierce," said Spurge. "He has carved up a whole . . . cohort of . . . goblin guards . . . with spinning blades. He's ruthless. . . . Aren't you? And a killer. . . . Of bad people."

Werfel agreed, "There are thousands who serve me and who are ready to rise up at my word."

"And you and your movement want to remove Ghohg the Evil One from power?"

"Most goblins do," Werfel answered, somewhat truthfully.

"And to accept the Elf King as your ruler and master?"

"If he will aid us," said Werfel, completely untruthfully.

"Then — tell me, you two. Tell me the secrets of the Well of Lightning." Clivers flipped through the pictures until he found a picture of the weird crystal spire. "These sketches were not exactly illuminating."

Spurge answered, "It's the source of much of the goblins' magical powers. It was brought here by Ghohg."

"Yes, but how does it work? Hm? Talk if you want to walk."

"It's not simple, my lord. . . ."

"You don't actually know, do you? You're just leading me on."

466

"Oh, no! It's just . . . it's not simple. It relies on a . . . Voortman helix. That is . . . mazzlicated . . . by the use of . . . frondings."

"Induperated frondings," Werfel agreed.

"Someone write this down," said Clivers. "I don't understand a word of it. You may remember, Weeds, I wasn't a particularly quick study when it came to the magical sciences."

"No, my lord. You spent most of those classes setting me on fire."

"Ah, yes. But you're still here, breathing and all. Well, briefly. No harm, no foul, Weedy. Continue."

"So that's how it creates energy. Through the . . . tension between the . . . magnetic chalice and . . . the . . . spin louvers." Then, in desperation: "Werfel knows more than me! He's an actual goblin!"

Werfel was also a better liar. "Yes, indeed, comrade Spurge. Thank you. You can read about the basic science behind the Voortman helix and the principles of a primitive spark spiral in Ellering's *On Zapping*. If you simply will deliver us to a library with a copy, we can show you —"

"Even better than Ellering," Spurge interrupted, "is Shelibar the Seven-Faced's *Powers and Energies of the Unseen World*."

"Yes, of course, Shelibar. Though my esteemed colleague

may not remember Mubiel's *Harnessing the Dark and Light.* Which is really much less superstitious than Shelibar."

"Ahem — but hardly necessary if you've read all the way to the end of *The Book of Ten Thousand Pages.* Maybe not something available in goblin libraries, but certainly available in the superior collections of the elves."

And the two scholars were off, reciting titles — some of them real, most of them made up — endless titles — until Clivers looked either bored or satisfied. (It was difficult to tell.)

"So there you have it," said Werfel. "The secrets of the Well of Lightning. Now the elves can build their own."

Spurge said, "Thank you for the opportunity to explain, my lord. I was worried my feeble transmissions could not convey the whole complexity of the energy-making process."

"We have so much more we can tell you," said Werfel. "So many things for you to learn. About the underground rivers that lead straight into the heart of Tenebrion, and the spells we goblins use to turn into bats."

"And the giant hands the goblins ride across the desert," Spurge added. "So much. But could we first get perhaps a sandwich?"

Ysoret Clivers rose. He dusted off his robes of priceless damask.

"No," he said. "You both will die."

Spurge yelled, "But we helped you!"

"Exactly. What you know is written down now. We'll look it up later in those books you just told me about. You are no longer useful, my little Weed." He began pulling on a glove. "Except for one thing: We plan to execute you just before dawn. That way we can take your head to the meeting with Ghohg. We can show him that you were not really our spy. After all, we wouldn't kill our own spy, would we?" Clivers bowed slightly. "And the goblin's head, too."

Spurge babbled, "You can't — why kill the goblin? Please, my lord. He's innocent of . . . No! Why would the king of the goblins want a goblin's head?"

"You just told me, Magister Spurge, that this is the leader of the Goblin Resistance. Thank you for delivering him to us. We've been worried about a worthwhile gift for Ghohg the Evil One. We were going to hand him some old, janky sword. But what would be better to open negotiations than the severed head of his own enemy?"

Spurge, red with rage, yelled, "You, Ysoret Clivers, are a —" And then he called Clivers all the names he'd been storing up for all the years. He shouted them, the veins standing out in his forehead.

Clivers just stood, smiling faintly, and listened. Then he mused, "How strange to think, little Weed, all those years ago in school . . . What if someone had told us that I'd be executing you and handing your head to a foreign king? We wouldn't have believed it."

Spurge whispered, "I would have, Clivers."

Clivers quirked his mouth. "Not the part about your head actually being internationally important. Who could have predicted that?"

With that, Ysoret Clivers, Lord Spymaster, left the tent.

Aghast, the two scholars waited for their deaths at dawn.

Chapter

02

In the dark of that night, Werfel and Brangwain Spurge thought about death. They sat in their cage, alone and without light.

They could not sleep because it was their last night alive. They wanted to see things, even if all they could see was dim lights carried past the canvas tent, glowing with a faint yellow warmth. They wanted to hear things, even if all they could hear was the clank of armor and the singing of crickets out in the wide elfin fields. They wanted to gather as much life as they could.

At around two or three in the morning, Werfel said, "We're not getting out, are we?"

"I have been thinking of plans, but we are in a metal cage, and this tent is surrounded by agents of the Order. I do not think we shall escape."

"Your idea about getting away from the ogre by sledding on that rusted shield was a very good one. You saved us both that day."

"You saved me many times, Archivist."

"We had some adventures. . . ." Werfel smiled sadly. "The fire . . . the bandits . . . I still cannot believe that you defeated Regibald du Burgh in single combat. You were smart to lure him up into that broken glass tower."

"But then — my foolishness in insulting him in the first place."

"Yes, that was somewhat foolish."

"It is a shame that our ride down through the city in the sphere was so frightening. I wish I could do that again sometime for fun." Spurge dreamed, "Maybe a sport . . . with two spheres rolling toward each other . . . And goalposts . . ."

"That would be fun."

"All things would be possible, if only we were going to live. But I have trapped both of us."

"Yes, you have."

"I have condemned us both to death."

"That's true. You really have."

"Archivist Werfel, I could never tell you how sorry I am."

Werfel thought long and hard. He was weighing something in his mind. When he had made his decision, he said, "Magister Spurge, once my esteemed guest, allow me to say: You are an idiot. An absolute idiot."

Spurge drew in a breath, indignant. "Now, wait. I —"

And then he realized what Werfel had just said.

Spurge felt a lump in his throat. He said, "Archivist, did you just call me . . . ?"

"Yes, Brangwain Spurge. No longer 'treasured.' No longer 'valued guest.' You are the biggest idiot I have ever met."

Spurge seized Werfel's hand and shook it. It was as if, imprisoned in that cage, a cage within his own heart had burst open. Someone cared about him. Despite everything, someone actually cared. "Oh, thank you," he said, and tears of gratitude ran down his cheeks. "Thank you, my ugly, misshapen, toad-like friend."

Werfel patted him on the hand and said with affection, "Don't touch me, you clammy, sweaty pedant."

"Nor you me, you squat, filthy bore! Your outfit is ridiculous and your beard is filled with twigs."

"Oh," said Werfel, flapping his arms, "to think I shall die wearing these stupid doll-print sheets!"

"Moron!"

"Goon!"

They laughed through their tears.

And so the two felt a little better, a little less alone when the executioner pulled aside the flap of the tent and announced that it was the hour of death: he was taking them to be slain, so their severed, bloody heads could be delivered to Ghohg, the goblin king.

It was time to die.

The Order's executioner unlocked the cage. "All right," he said. "Come on. We'll chop quickly."

The two scholars rose stiffly. They ducked out the door of the cage.

The executioner backed away from them, holding his pike at the ready in case one of them tried to escape.

He did not notice the small form that had fluttered in after him.

Skardebek.

The icthyod hung back in the shadows of the tent until she saw that Werfel was free.

Then she darted forward and clamped herself angrily over the executioner's hooded face. He gagged and clutched at her. First with one hand, then with both hands.

Spurge rushed forward and grabbed his pike as it fell.

The executioner stumbled to his knees, tearing at his own face.

Skardebek flapped away — and Spurge slammed the guard over the head with the pike. The man collapsed.

Spurge took the executioner's chain-mail tunic and the black hood. He and Werfel fumbled with the man's wide belt. They tied it around Spurge's scrawny middle. They pulled the hood down low over Spurge's face.

Then they walked out of the tent with Spurge disguised, forcing Werfel before him, jabbing him in the neck with the pike.

The agents from the Order of the Clean Hand did not object. They knew the prisoners were going to be taken for execution.

The camp was eerie in those hollow hours of early morning. It was dark, and sounds were muffled. Giant iron baskets held burning logs to light the rows of white tents. Squires sat, half asleep, near griffin steeds, making sure the animals were fed and ready. From the tents came the snoring of knights and foot soldiers. Dukes and earls had rich rugs spread on the grass before their tents, with their shields hung up on display.

"Look!" whispered Spurge. He pointed across a parade ground.

In a pavilion of colored silk, the Elf King was being dressed for his meeting by fifteen servants. He was standing with his arms out straight while they draped him with ermine, velvet, samite, brocade, and cloth of gold. Two maidens with braids of silver held the royal crown.

The two scholars stared in wonder.

Guards looked over their way. Quickly, the two started off again through the alleys of tents, past the pavilions of elfin lords.

They got all the way to the edge of the camp before anyone noticed them. Then, there, where the tents met the dark of night, they were challenged.

"Who's that?" said a picket guard. His lantern illuminated their faces. "A goblin? Why are you —"

Spurge panicked and swung the pike wildly. The guard brought up his sword. The two clashed. Spurge didn't know what he was doing.

Another guard, alerted by the noise, ran over. "What's going on?" he demanded, seeing the two elves fighting.

Spurge blurted, "This guard is an imposter! Help me seize him!"

The trick worked for only a second. The newcomer tried to figure out what was happening, eyes wide under his helmet — which was just long enough for Werfel to jump on him from the side. The two went down. Werfel grabbed his weapon. He shoved his hand over the man's mouth.

"I apologize deeply for this indignity," Werfel said as he knelt on the newcomer's chest.

The other tried to scream for help, but Skardebek flapped in his face and he choked. He raised up his gloved hand to fend off the icthyod, and Spurge took the opportunity to belt the guard in the stomach. The picket guard fell backward, the breath knocked out of him.

They left the two guards gagged and tied with their own cloaks and ran into the wilderness at the foot of the Bonecruel Mountains. Over the jagged peaks, the sky turned green.

They had escaped the elfin camp.

It was almost dawn.

Chapter 04

From Lord Spymaster Ysoret Clivers,
Order of the Clean Hand
To His Royal Highness, the King of Elfland

Your Highness,

This note simply to tell you quickly that I shall be along
in a moment to accompany you to the parley with the Evil
One. As you've doubtless heard, there's just a slight delay, a
wee delay getting the heads of the two prisoners to give to
Ghohg. The Order are searching the camp for the escapees,
and we shall appear with the heads in perhaps a quarter of
an hour.

Aha! Here is your Royal Champion now — doubtless to escort me to your side. Let me send him with this note back to your —

I see. That is not why the Royal Champion is here at all. I understand, Your Maj, that you are upset that the prisoners have just temporarily escaped, but I give you my word of honor that

your majesty really this is

you do realize your maj that I only have two fingers left on the right hand and it is

now I do call this unfair your maj

will you please tell your

just give me a few minutes and

I shall be at your side with

I must object in the strongest possible

Chapter

65

Spurge, Werfel, and Skardebek were fleeing back into the Bonecruel Mountains. They didn't have a goal or a plan. They just wanted to get away from the elfin camp before the sun rose too high.

They struggled through bushes. Distant fanfares sounded.

As they groped their way past giant boulders, using their stolen pikes as walking sticks, Werfel cranked his spectacles to maximum magnification and looked back down the slope.

"What's happening?" Spurge asked.

Werfel handed the magnifiers to his friend. "The Elf King is coming out of his pavilion. It looks like they're getting ready for him to go meet Ghohg."

Spurge peered through the spectacles. "Yes. He's getting on a griffin. There's his herald carrying his golden umbrella. . . . And there's . . . Clivers. Oh, Clivers."

A few minutes later, the two scholars looked up from their climb to watch the three griffins flying up a nearby slope, carrying the royal party. Banners of white samite flapped in the air. The sky was growing brighter.

In another twenty minutes, the two scholars came upon another vantage point. They looked down at the camp below them. All the elfin knights and soldiers had turned out, and they were standing in their battle ranks, ready for action if something went wrong.

Then Werfel traced the line of the mountains upward. His gaze reached a flat summit covered in grass. There he saw the three royal griffins tied to stakes, grazing.

"Magister!" he hissed. "Magister! The king and his party are walking forward, under the ceremonial parasol. . . ."

On the other side of the summit, Ghohg hovered, surrounded by a glowing corona. He had two goblins to attend him.

The Elf King strode forward. Ghohg moved to meet him.

The two scholars breathlessly handed the magnifying spectacles back and forth.

"We are witnessing history," said Spurge. "If only we could hear their parley!"

"What's happening, Magister?"

The two leaders stood facing each other, about forty feet apart. Then Lord Ysoret Clivers started forward, and a goblin minister marched toward him from the other side. It was time for the exchange of ceremonial gifts.

Spurge said, "Clivers is ... He's proffering a gift. Some kind of a sword. The goblin is bowing. The goblin takes the sword. He has some kind of a box with Ghohg's gift to the Elf King. He's opening it ... taking out ..." Spurge yelped. He thrust the lenses toward Werfel.

Werfel grabbed them.

Winking in the first light of dawn, held in the hands of the goblin emissary, was the gemstone Spurge had brought to Tenebrion.

Werfel cackled. "Well, there's a slap in the face of the Elf King! Ghohg is returning your gift! Ha! To show he's displeased! What an insult!"

They couldn't wait to see what happened next.

What happened was that Ysoret Clivers looked terrified. Absolutely panic-stricken. And yet the goblin still approached him, holding out the gemstone. The goblin bowed and handed it to the horrified Lord Spymaster.

And so the elfin gift was returned by the kingdom of the goblins.

Chapter

66

Top Secret
Transmission

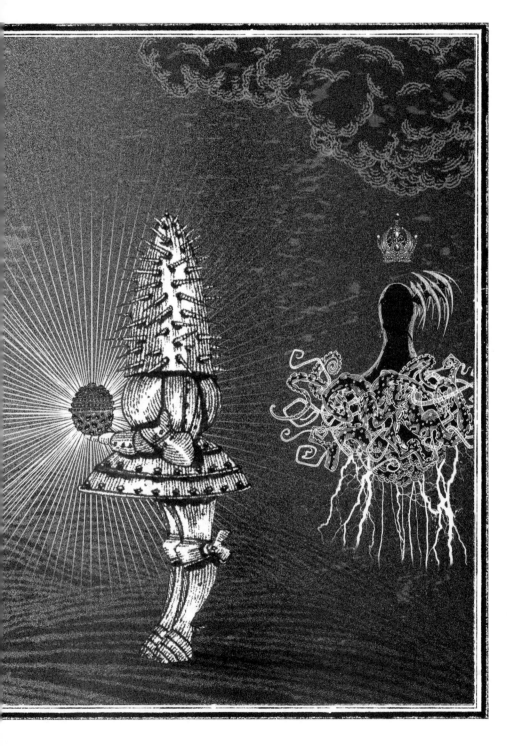

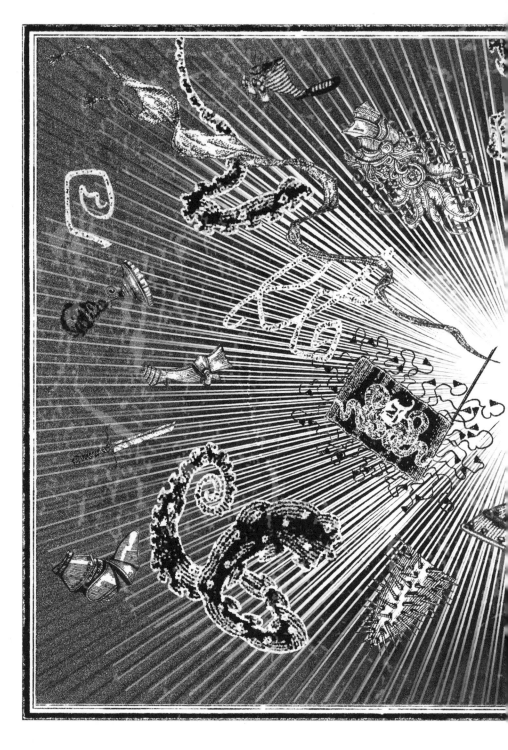

Chapter

67

The wind roared past them. They gripped rocks. Skardebek, shrieking, was being sucked away. Spurge reached out and grabbed her. The scholars bowed their heads before the blast.

After the explosion blew a hole in time and space, the air rushed into it, taking with it boulders and dirt and trees shot like arrows into the void. Though the blast was two miles away, Werfel was terrified that it would continue to swallow the world, league by league, until nothing was left. He braced himself against the rock of the mountains and clamped his eyes shut. The bright image of the explosion still flared against his eyelids while the howling wind blocked every other sound except the angry yipping of Skardebek, clutched to Spurge's chest, furious at the storm all around them.

Then, as quickly as it was opened up, the tear in the world closed.

The wind died down. The clouds slowed. When the elf and the goblin looked up again, all that was left of the summit where the two kings had met was a spherical hole, smoking.

The column of smoke was thick as mud.

"What was that?" whispered Werfel.

"A bomb," said Spurge. His face was white with shock. "The gemstone was a bomb. They tricked me. They wanted me to deliver a bomb to Tenebrion without even knowing it."

"The Elf King and the Protector . . . both gone," said Werfel in awe, gaping at the slow turning of the smoke. "Our leaders are both gone."

"I must go into my trance and send pictures."

"Hmm? Why, Spurge? The people who hired you are gone."

"Because, Archivist, I am a historian. The elves of Dwelholm need to know what really happened here. You and I are the only two people to witness, up close, the most momentous political event to occur in the last thousand years."

Werfel thought about it and agreed. "You will make history. Scholars in the future will look at these pictures."

"And I must correct the ones I already sent. But there's no time for that right now."

"No," said Werfel. "Soon our two peoples will start blaming each other for this explosion."

"Indeed, Archivist. And then the bloodshed will start."

Werfel shook his head with concern. "We must stop it."

"As quickly as possible."

Werfel sat heavily upon a boulder. "It is unimaginable," he said. "A thousand years ago, your race flew out of the west, riding on griffins, and conquered us. Your royal line was founded by your warlord back then, and lasted until this morning. Five hundred years ago, Ghohg the Protector arrived from another world to rule us. Today, everything our peoples have known for the last thousand years has been erased."

"The past is not erased, Archivist," said Spurge wisely. "But the future is changed."

"And we will be here to watch," said Werfel with excitement. "We will witness history, and we will write it. We will do our small part to tell people, 'This is what you should know about the way our kingdoms were ruled.'"

"Perhaps, in a thousand years," said Spurge with a smile, "our books — books with our names upon them — will be the ones idiots like us will argue over."

"So let us begin, Magister Spurge!"

508

"I will, Archivist, if you will just shut up!"

"What images will you send?"

And so, at once excited, and anxious, and confused, and certain, the two scholars planned out the images Spurge would send back to the Order of the Clean Hand. They talked about the Elf King and his ceremonial umbrella, and Ghohg's spiky emissary. They described to each other the tumbling gem.

By noon, confused patrols were flying over the mountains. Griffin-riders spied angry wyverns and swerved away, unclear as to whether they were all at war.

Far below the screeching griffins, on a mountaintop, a tiny goblin archivist and an icthyod basked in the sun, and beside them, a scholar elf hovered above the wildflowers, crackling with energy; and he sent through the bright air the newest chapter in the story of the botched and bungled assassination of Brangwain Spurge.

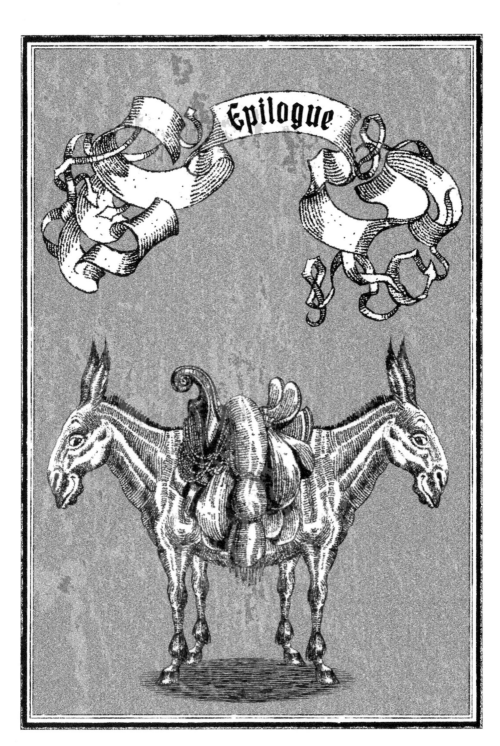

A week later, the two scholars were riding through the Bonecruel Mountains. They rode two-headed donkeys because they frequently needed to change direction.

Everything was in chaos. No one knew who was ruling Elfland or the kingdom of the goblins. In the capitals, people shouted about government and the future. In Dwelholm, various elfin noblemen claimed that they had a drop of King Degravaunt's blood running through their blue veins from fifteen generations back. Others tried to poison them. In Tenebrion, there was a Council of Goblins that was trying to decide the future of the nation while different groups shoved and fought for power: the War Party, the Peace Party, the Party of the Eastern Sludge, the Mountaintop Pioneers' Party, the People's Party, the Party of Princes — all of them claiming to save Tenebrion from disaster.

Meanwhile, Spurge and Werfel spent their time going back and forth, carrying messages between the nations. They were some of the only people who could speak both the language of elves and of goblins. More important, everywhere they went, they had to keep explaining the weird set of mistakes and missteps and deceptions that had caused the destruction of both rulers. Otherwise, the elves would blame the goblins and the goblins would blame the elves, and the thousand years of war would simply start again. Spurge and Werfel were tired of telling the story. It was hard to convince some people, though. So many wanted to have someone to hate, someone to fight. It was all Spurge and Werfel could do to convince their kingdoms to sort out their own problems instead of striking out in rage and hysterical fear.

"If only everyone would read Archivist Werfel's new pamphlet 'On Prosperity and Peace,' " said Spurge.

"Or Magister Brangwain Spurge's 'An Elfin Way Forward,' " said Werfel.

"Though of course," said Spurge, "Werfel's book is boring."

"And Spurge's is best used for lighting fires," said Werfel.

The mountains were filled with mist. Skardebek was sitting on Werfel's shoulder, licking her wings.

Spurge scratched his arms as he rode. "I believe I am allergic to goblins," he said.

"Once I wondered whether you were allergic to small hospitality chocolates."

"I have not stopped itching for days. Since I slept in poison ivy."

"I do not think you slept in poison ivy," Werfel hinted.

"What does my mysterious friend mean?"

Werfel just smiled.

When Spurge said, "Pull out the cork, Werfel. What's going on?", Werfel answered, "I think you may have more goblin in you than you think."

"What does that mean?"

"Let us stop these two-headed donkeys."

They stopped and dismounted. Then Werfel said, "Have you noticed your scalp peeling?"

"Not as much as I have noticed your warts, carbuncles, and runny nose."

"I am not joking, Spurge."

Spurge kept scratching. And scratching. Little flakes of skin fell off. And then larger flakes of skin fell off.

"This is very strange," said Spurge.

"But a very exciting moment for my ignorant friend," said Werfel.

Spurge kept scratching at his skin while Werfel went to their baskets of provisions and pulled out an eel-pickle pie and a bottle of gorgonbladder wine. He opened the wine and poured two glasses full.

It was not yet dinnertime, but among friends — friends who want to change the world together — new beginnings always call for a celebration.

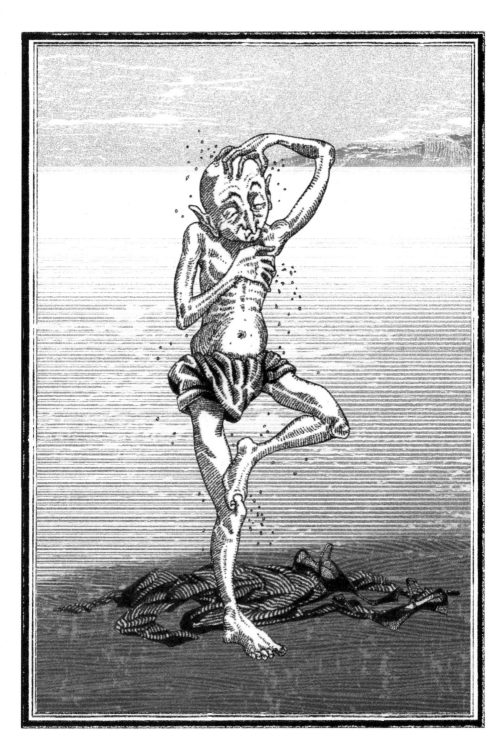

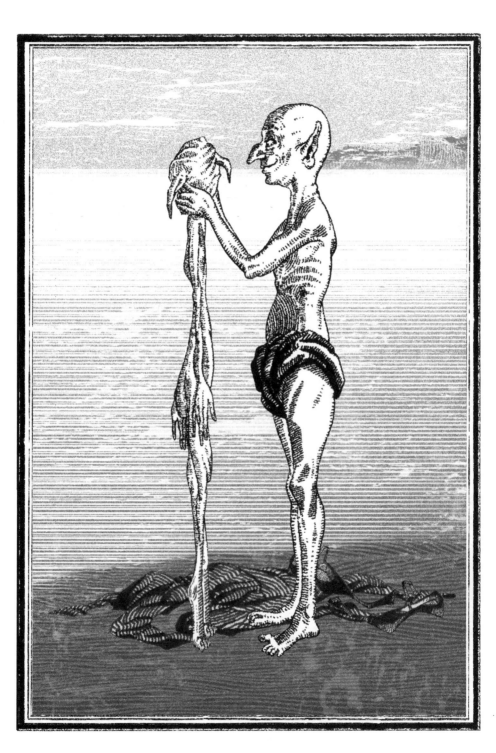

AUTHORS' NOTE

M. T. ANDERSON: A word about how we created this book may be of interest to readers who also write and draw their own stories. Usually an author will write the text, then an illustrator will draw pictures to match that text. But in this case, Eugene had a fascinating idea.

EUGENE YELCHIN: I wanted to work on a book in which the pictures wouldn't illustrate the text like they normally do. Instead they would actually *disagree* with it. They would tell a very different story.

MTA: The words and the pictures would be at war.

EY: Ah, war! A terrible thing, but so fun to draw. Swords, axes, beheadings . . .

MTA: I loved Eugene's idea and was extremely excited to get a chance to work with a genius like Eugene, even if everybody warned me that he was sometimes sort of difficult.

EY: And everybody warned me that M. T. Anderson was a grumpy nerd who basically lived in the fourteenth century.

MTA: So I began sending Eugene ideas until he liked one. It took a long time, but it was worth it.

EY: For whom?

MTA: We kept batting ideas back and forth. What we arrived at finally was a story about a bookish, somewhat meek, maybe even uptight elfin historian trying to describe the culture of the goblins. He would misunderstand the wonders and terrors he saw, the mysteries of a society very different from his own. He would send home images full of errors.

EY: Speaking of errors, you should've read the letters I was writing home when I came to America from Russia!

MTA: Exactly.

EY: What do you mean, exactly? You didn't read them.

MTA: Of course, Eugene, I didn't. But, anyway, the great thing about writing a story with a friend is that you push each other to go places you wouldn't have even thought of if you were working alone.

EY: Avoid those places like the plague. You'll never get out of there alive. And would you really call us "friends"?

MTA: I mean, we've only actually spent a half an hour together. And it was not great. But our readers should know that the important thing when you're working with someone else is to be open to whatever direction they suggest.

EY: Really? However insane it might be?

MTA: So Eugene and I created this book as a tribute to all of those brave writer-explorers in the ancient world who voyaged into unknown lands and tried to understand the cultures they found there: Marco Polo, Herodotus, Ibn Battuta, Xuanzang, Sir John Mandeville, and Faxian.

EY: What are you talking about? This is a spy thriller. Murder! Chases! Double crosses! We got a bomb in there!

MTA: But, Eugene, at its heart, it's really a tragic meditation on how societies that have been trained to hate each other for generations can actually come to see eye to eye.

EY: A tragedy, my eye! A crazy story about two fools blinded by propaganda is not a tragedy. It's a comedy.

MTA: Sure, Eugene, whatever. Basically, we just wondered why goblins get such a bad rap in fantasy novels like J. R. R. Tolkien's *Lord of the Rings*. Why are goblins always seen as faceless grunts who deserve to be slaughtered? What would it actually be like to live in the barren realm of an oppressive dark lord?

EY: Who's Tolkien? Never heard of him. I hate fantasy.

MTA: Is this discussion over? I have a dentist appointment.

EY: My first root canal was done by a KGB dentist in Siberia without anesthetic.

MTA: Are we finished?

EY: Wait! Anderson! Where are you going? I'm just getting started....

M. T. Anderson is the author of *Feed,* winner of the *Los Angeles Times* Book Prize; the National Book Award–winning *The Astonishing Life of Octavian Nothing, Traitor to the Nation, Volume I: The Pox Party* and its sequel, *The Kingdom on the Waves,* both *New York Times* bestsellers and Michael L. Printz Honor Books; *Symphony for the City of the Dead: Dmitri Shostakovich and the Siege of Leningrad; Landscape with Invisible Hand;* and many other books for children and young adults. He lives near Boston, Massachusetts.

Eugene Yelchin is a Russian-American author and illustrator of many books for children, including *Breaking Stalin's Nose,* a Newbery Honor Book; *The Haunting of Falcon House,* a Golden Kite Award winner; and *The Rooster Prince of Breslov,* a National Jewish Book Award winner. He has also received the Society of Children's Book Writers and Illustrators' Tomie dePaola Award. He lives with his wife and two children in Topanga, California.

To Tarquin, Dot, and LaRue,
who I think would really love this book
if they were human — M. T. A.

In memory of Anton — E. Y.

Text copyright © 2018 by M. T. Anderson
Illustrations copyright © 2018 by Eugene Yelchin

First edition 2018

Library of Congress Catalog Card Number pending
ISBN 978-0-7636-9822-5

18 19 20 21 22 23 TSH 10 9 8 7 6 5 4 3 2 1

Printed in Dexter, MI, U.S.A.

This book was typeset in Historical Fell Type and Tiepolo.
The illustrations were done in pen and ink and assembled digitally.

Candlewick Press
99 Dover Street
Somerville, Massachusetts 02144

visit us at www.candlewick.com